OUTLAW TRAIL

E. E. HALLERAN

WHEELER
CHIVERS

This Large Print edition is published by Wheeler Publishing, Waterville, Maine, USA and by BBC Audiobooks Ltd, Bath, England.
Wheeler Publishing, a part of Gale, Cengage Learning.
The text of this Large Print edition is unabridged.
Other aspects of the book may vary from the original edition.
Set in 16 pt. Plantin.
Printed on permanent paper.

LIBRARY OF CONGRESS CATALOGING-IN-PUBLICATION DATA

Halleran, E. E. (Eugene E.), 1905–
   Outlaw trail / by E. E. Halleran.
     p. cm. — (Wheeler Publishing large print western)
     ISBN-13: 978-1-59722-906-7 (pbk. : alk. paper)
     ISBN-10: 1-59722-906-7 (pbk. : alk. paper)
     1. Outlaws—Fiction. 2. Large type books. I. Title.
 PS3515.A3818O94 2005
 813'.54—dc22   2008045592

BRITISH LIBRARY CATALOGUING-IN-PUBLICATION DATA AVAILABLE

Published in 2009 in the U.S. by arrangement with Golden West Literary Agency.
Published in 2009 in the U.K. by arrangement with Golden West Literary Agency.

U.K. Hardcover: 978 1 408 43266 2 (Chivers Large Print)
U.K. Softcover: 978 1 408 43267 9 (Camden Large Print)

OUTLAW TRAIL

1

Sunrise was always a belated event in Tinaja. Long after the first wisps of daylight had drifted across the valley a reluctant sun would scale the ragged heights of the Javelinas, turning the gray of half light into the full glare of border sunshine. Not that anyone complained. There was little enough about Tinaja that would stand extra light. In the course of a short but violent career, the town had managed to pick up most of the bad features of other frontier communities, at the same time avoiding the virtues which generally crept into the lives of other towns. It was just a collection of adobes, sheet iron shacks, and unpainted frame buildings, the sort of place to shelter the fugitive, the saddle bum, the adventurer, the outcast. Perhaps it was just as well that the sun did not spill its searching rays across Tinaja's dirtiness any sooner than it did. An extra hour of peace and semi-darkness was something of a mercy.

It was into this brief interval of dim quiet that Pegleg Clancy thrust his wrinkled countenance, sniffing eagerly from behind the batwings of the Palo Duro Saloon. Pegleg practically lived for this part of the morning, an hour he had come to think of as his own private property. Since cracking up as a cowhand he had been forced to take whatever employment came his way — and he had never managed to accustom himself to the smells that went with the chore of swamping out the Palo Duro. In Pegleg's opinion, whisky was all right in its place but he couldn't get enthusiastic about it when it was just a stale odor mingled with other assorted smells of horses, leather, body-sweat, dead seegars, and all too often the reek of burned gunpowder.

Leaving the batwings fanning gently behind him, he crossed the hard-packed dirt sidewalk to the hitching rack and leaned there, easing his aching stump in its ill-fitting peg and hooking his one good arm around the rail to support his warped body. Then he took a deep, deliberate breath, expelling the foul air which he had been taking into his lungs while cleaning out the Palo Duro's latest accumulation of debris. Pegleg was not a finicky soul but he had learned to hate his job for its constant odors.

It was good to be out in the open air after a session with broom and mop, good to be away from the sour reeks of dead revelry. It was pleasant to forget the dim barroom and to look out across the rolling browns of the valley, resting his eyes on the dark, serrated line of the Javelina crests. Soon the rising sun would turn the spiny ridge into just another range of mountains, gray, green and brown like other hills, but now it was restfully dark, silhouetted sharply against the red of the approaching day. That was the way Clancy liked it, the way he knew it as something which was his alone.

Every morning for months he had been going through this routine of leaving his chores for a brief look at the world he had once known so much better, making a ritual of it until somehow it eased the bitterness which swept his mind so much of the time. In this hour the world was his. There was no one to bother him, no one to call him names nor to order him about. The solitude almost made a man forget. At least it helped him to remember without bitterness the days when he had been a whole man and not a pathetic bundle of badly healed injuries. He could almost forget the way Chandler Brack had discarded him after

9

that accident at Circle D.

Consequently it was with a feeling of vague resentment that the little swamper saw a rider swinging into the untidy main street. For a moment Clancy knew only a dull anger that anyone should come along to spoil his brief moment of contentment, then a quick interest drove away the more unpleasant emotion. Pegleg was still enough of a range hand to be observing, and he promptly spotted a couple of points that were odd enough to capture his full attention.

For one thing the newcomer was a striking picture in complete black, a black-clad rider on a black horse, the sombre note relieved only by a generous twinkle of silver in the accouterments and on the stranger's big cone-shaped sombrero. Snap judgment told Pegleg that this was a vaquero dandy coming to town, but just as quickly he knew that the guess was not good enough. The black one did not sit his bronc in the manner of a casual traveler; there was a purpose in his attitude, a purpose Clancy could sense without being able to explain. A man who has known bitterness sometimes can recognize it in others without actually knowing the reason for the recognition. So it was with Pegleg Clancy. This fancy newcomer had the appearance of a swashbuckling young Latin on a holiday. But Clancy would have offered odds that the tall figure in the ornate saddle was tense with bitter emotion.

The little man tried to tell himself that he was imagining things but then he realized something else. This stranger was coming into town from the north, the blind end of the Javelina basin. There wasn't much of anything up that way except the encircling ring of abrupt mountains, no ranches where a traveler could have remained overnight, no trails which would have offered any normal route into Tinaja. Yet this man was not dusty nor trail-worn. His tight-fitting black garments looked fresh and new. The silver-trimmed black sombrero was almost shiny in its newness, while the long-legged black stallion was too glossy for belief. Both the man and the horse seemed to have stepped right out of the groomer's hands.

Clancy let a crooked, bony forefinger run idly across the side of his wizened cheek, absently tracing out the scar which marked the cheekbone. "That's dam' funny," he muttered. "Wonder where that jigger popped up from all spick and span? Seems like he musta built hisself outa thin air. Either that or he just swung down outa the

11

Sierra Verdes, which shore ain't likely."

By that time the stranger was within fifty yards. Either he did not see Pegleg hunched there under the saloon's wooden awning, or he pretended that he did not. Certainly he offered no greeting. Without even glancing around at the sorry drabness of Tinaja he dismounted swiftly, his long, lean body flowing in lines of easy grace as he strode toward the nearest building, a rectangle of cardboard in his left hand. Pegleg was not sure, but he thought the cardboard had been drawn from beneath the black rider's shirt. It was certain that he had not been carrying it openly while he was in the saddle, but now he seemed almost to flaunt it as he crossed the dirt sidewalk to the door of the express company's office.

Something nagged at Clancy's memory. Somehow the black stranger seemed familiar, but Pegleg could not tell why. He watched while the man tacked his placard to the office door, using the handle of a shiny dagger as a tack hammer. Then, without any wasted motion, the stranger was back in the saddle again, angling across the street toward the Miners' Bank, a squat, brick building which almost directly faced the Palo Duro and the interested Pegleg Clancy.

12

This time the performance was slightly different. Another poster appeared in the man's hand as he dismounted, and this time Pegleg knew that it had indeed come from inside the neatly pressed black shirt. Judging by the faint bulge there was still another one in reserve. The stranger varied his action a little now, shoving the cardboard under the door of the bank instead of tacking it up in plain view.

Only when he had remounted did he seem to become aware of the crooked little man watching him from across the street. For just a split second he stared from beneath crisp black brows, then he bowed politely, raising a lean hand in greeting as he swung the black horse away from the bank. *"Salud, amigo,"* he said softly, his words coming in precise tones which brought that same elusive hint of memory to Pegleg's mind. He was sure he had never heard anyone talk like that — and yet he had.

"Howdy," Clancy replied, frowning hard over his effort to identify the stranger. He had known a lot of Mexicans since coming here to the border country, but he could not recall one of quite this fellow's proportions. Tall, thin ones were not uncommon, not even tall ones with such carefully trimmed mustaches and tiny imperials, but

13

he couldn't make this dandy fit into any particular class. He was almost too fancy.

By that time the fellow was moving away, and Clancy had a new view of him — a view which jogged the dim memory still further. Seen from the rear it was clear that the man was not as thin as he had first appeared. Maybe his height or the tight black shirt had been responsible for the illusion, but now Pegleg knew that the stranger's breadth of shoulder was rather notable. And even that seemed to stir the reluctant sense of familiarity.

The old swamper was still frowning when the Mexican halted for a third time, practically repeating his actions of the first stop as he tacked a third placard on one of the posts supporting the ramshackle awning of the old Gem Saloon. Which was a mite peculiar, Clancy thought. Anyone with half an eye could see that the Palo Duro was a bigger place than the Gem, a better location for a public notice than the older saloon. Why then should the poster have been placed in the less prominent spot? Could it be that the black rider had chosen the Gem because no one had been lounging in front of it? Had he deliberately avoided close contact with Pegleg Clancy?

The sound of a footfall from somewhere

in his rear caught Clancy's attention. A squatty, unshaven man in corduroy pants and a dirty undershirt had come out from between the Palo Duro and the adjoining hardware store to stare interestedly at the departing stranger. The fringe of bushy gray hair which framed his shining bald spot was bristling in all directions, joining with the stubbly chin to make him look completely unkempt.

"What's goin' on, Pegleg?" the dumpy man asked, rubbing at sleepy eyes with one hand while he tamped rough-cut into a blackened pipe with the opposite thumb.

Clancy did not resent the name. Everyone was calling him that nowadays, and Ben Arms didn't mean any more by it than the rest of them did. Ben was decent enough in his own lazy, offhand manner. Maybe he didn't run his hardware store in a very efficient manner, but he wasn't always pushing a man around like some folks Clancy could have named.

"A big Mex jigger jest slapped up a couple o' posters," Clancy told him. "Mebbe we oughta take a look-see." He unhooked his good arm from the hitch rail and moved crab fashion toward the express office, saying no more as Ben Arms fell in beside him. For a moment or so there was only the subdued squeak of Ben's corduroys, and then Arms inquired, "Did ye know the critter?"

"Nope." Clancy was short with his answer. For some reason he could not have explained even to himself, he was not ready to mention the fact that there had been something perplexingly familiar about the black rider.

Arms lighted his pipe, puffed a couple of times, and grumbled, "Funny kind of a caper fer a Mex. Mostly they're dodgin' posters, not postin' them. I remember one —"

Pegleg interrupted hastily. He was too familiar with Ben Arms' habit of talking volubly about nothing to let himself in for one of those vocal onslaughts. "Might be border patrol business," he suggested. "They're workin' kinda queer combinations nowadays."

"Could be," Arms allowed. He probably would have made oral capital of that lead, only the two men were now squarely in front of the poster which adorned the express office door. They studied it intently for several minutes, neither of them speaking until they had spelled out the words with due care. It was the familiar type of lawman's notice, but Clancy's alert eye

16

caught an oddity here just as he had spotted the queer feature in the mysterious rider's approach to Tinaja. The announcement was simple enough. The authorities of El Paso wanted a bandit known as El Diablo Negro. The outlaw was charged with robbery of a stagecoach, and it was specified that he must be taken alive. Evidently the El Paso folks didn't require his arrest too urgently for the reward mentioned was a mere five hundred dollars. The outlaw was described as being a tall Mexican, swarthy and lightly built, inclined to considerable vanity in attire and addicted to the wearing of black clothing. Hence the name by which he had recently become notorious.

That much was routine. The odd part was that the poster had apparently been used before. It showed tinges of yellow at the edges and three of its corners showed old tack holes while the upper left corner had been ripped off entirely.

"So old Diablo's on the loose again, hey?" Ben Arms muttered, puffing vigorously at the rough-cut which was already giving off an acrid cloud of smoke. "I ain't heard tell o' that rascal fer a couple o' years now. Wonder how come they figger he'll turn up in this part o' the hills?"

Suddenly his complacency changed to

17

sharp interest. "Say! I seen enough o' that rider to know that he was all rigged out in black. Just like Diablo always was. Yuh don't figger it would be —"

"Description fits," Clancy told him, stepping back away from the noxious fumes that were coming from Ben's pipe. "It coulda been Black Devil hisself what put up the sign, only why would a bandit want to go around postin' up reward notices fer hisself?"

Arms reached a heavy paw over one shoulder, scratching perplexedly at the slack of his undershirt. "Some damn queer things happen in Tinaja. Like old Turkle marryin' that Mamie Rook. Who woulda figgered —"

Clancy cut him off hastily. "Wonder where that feller got to so dad-blamed fast? He was right there at the end o' the street and headin' south. Now he's outa sight."

"Mebbe he cut back toward the Sierra Verdes," Arms suggested. He lumbered away between the buildings, showing considerable agility for one of his short coupled bulk. Clancy hobbled along a few yards until he could see the rolling valley to the east. There was no rider in sight in that direction.

The hardware dealer returned quickly enough, his broad face wrinkled into a questioning frown. "He ain't showin' on that side. Ye shore enough seen him go outa town?"

"I figured he did. And he ain't over toward the Javelinas neither."

Arms laughed shortly. "Plumb mysterious. Only there's plenty o' ridges just west o' town. He could be headin' fer the Verdes and easy be outa sight already."

"Likely," Clancy assented. "But it's some peculiar. He appeared like outa thin air so it ain't no use stretchin' the imagination to think he disappeared the same way."

Arms frowned again, evidently puzzled at the little man's tone. Pegleg said no more, however, letting his mind buzz over that elusive memory which kept coming back to him. There had been something plenty familiar about that Mexican's lean face and rangy build, something which Clancy knew he ought to recognize. But he couldn't quite make connections.

He thought about it while Arms rattled on in his usual aimless fashion. Suddenly he caught himself up with a start as the hardware dealer asked, "Ye didn't know the jigger, hey?"

For a moment Clancy wondered if his companion had been reading his thoughts, but as Arms rambled on without waiting for an answer he knew that it had been just a chance comment. Already Ben was going on with his gossip. "Not many fellers out here would be apt to know Diablo," he declared, a little importantly. "Over along the Rio Grande, though, he's some punkins with the peons. They plumb swear by old Diablo."

"Never heard of him," Clancy stated.

"El Diablo Negro." Arms let the name roll from his lips, evidently pleased at having an audience for his information. "The Mex Robin Hood in a black suit. Quite a feller. He always seems to —"

"Robin who?" Clancy interrupted.

Arms chuckled. "Robin Hood. A kind of English Sam Bass, if ye know what I mean. Plain hell on lawmen, but a right nice feller among his friends. He got hisself a reputation fer passin' out the loot to poor folks jest as fast as he steals it, and always pokin' his snoot into somebody else's business, mostly when there's a dirty job on hand that nobody else seems to be able to clean up. Right nice waddy fer a Mex, the boys along the Pecos useta say. I remember when —"

"How long ago did ye know him?" Clancy demanded, trying to shut off a yarn which probably would not be on the subject.

"I didn't know him. I jest heard about him

20

when I was workin' in El Paso. I had a job in a store there before I got smart and branched out fer myself. Worked fer an old coot named Judson. Seems like I heard he got killed a year or so ago."

"Judson?"

"No. Diablo."

"But ye never seen him?"

"Nope."

"Got any idea how old a galoot he would be?"

Arms thought about that one for a minute. "Mebbe forty. Why?"

"I'm jest curious." Pegleg couldn't have told anyone why he did not blurt out the thought which crossed his mind. For some reason he had a notion that the mysterious rider was deliberately trying to call attention to himself as El Diablo Negro. And he wasn't old enough to be the outlaw Arms had described. Clancy would have bet that the man he had just seen was not over thirty, probably a few years under that mark. Then why was he deliberately masquerading as an outlaw and trying to put lawmen on his own trail?

Ben Arms was still chattering volubly about Diablo's sudden appearance in Tinaja as the two men strolled back to their respective doors. In a sense his mind was running

21

parallel to Clancy's. It didn't make sense, Ben declared, for an outlaw to post signs offering a reward for his own arrest. Diablo must be going loco. Pegleg grunted non-committally and Arms went back into the alley which led to his back door, leaving a trail of smoke behind him.

Clancy stood still for a few moments, toying with his ideas and the irritating sense of thwarted memory, then he turned away from the Palo Duro's batwings and scuttled on down the dirt street, forcing his peg into brisk activity as he aimed for the Gem. Now that the morning had been ruined by the stranger's queer activities, and by Ben Arms' pipe, he might as well make a day of it.

The placard on the Gem made the weathered lines of his gaunt little face pucker into new wrinkles of perplexity. Here was another ordinary reward poster, advertising for the arrest of a payroll bandit believed to be the notorious El Diablo Negro. The outlaw was described as being thirty-five years of age, over six feet in height, slightly built, swarthy of complexion, and accustomed to the wearing of black clothing. Like the poster on the express office it was yellowed with age and exposure, its corners showing indications of previous tacking.

This time, however, it was the sheriff of Valencia County, New Mexico Territory, who displayed seven hundred and fifty dollars' worth of interest in the capture of the black one.

"Everything right but the age," Clancy muttered to himself. "What the hell is it all about?"

He wished that he might compare these two posters with the third one which had been shoved under the door of the Miners' Bank, but he knew that no one would have any look at that until eight-thirty. Promptly at that hour Chandler Brack would ride into Tinaja from his imposing ranch house in the foothills of the nearby Sierra Verdes, would bow pompously to those citizens considered worthy of the honor, and would unlock the double oak door of the bank building. He had been doing that every morning since attaining the degree of affluence which made him the local banker as well as owner of half of the basin's real estate.

Thought of Brack brought back some of the bitterness which Clancy had been forgetting but he forced it away, for the moment regretting only that it would be Chandler Brack who would get first look at that third poster. Somehow Clancy had an idea that the odd one would be of particular interest; otherwise it would have been tacked up in public like the others.

He went back to the Palo Duro then, suddenly aware that the Javelinas had changed their color. The sun was up, glowing redly above the castellated peaks and throwing long shadows across the rolling valley around Tinaja. Clancy shrugged a little, the bitterness sweeping back as he returned to the noisy interior of the saloon. Idle speculation might be interesting enough but it didn't put any dinero in a man's pockets. It was time to get back on the job, even such a miserable job as swamping out Chandler Brack's saloon.

2

Jabe Conree was not a particularly intelligent man in a lot of ways, but he knew cattle and he was smart enough to recognize the buttered side of his bread. These two qualities had made him a good foreman for Chandler Brack's growing cattle interests. The fact that he bossed the toughest crew in the territory made some folks think of him as a hard man, but those who knew the situation were not deceived. Conree was simply shrewd enough to give the orders and let somebody else see that they were carried out. It was Chandler Brack who supplied him with a cutthroat crew so he was entirely willing to let a Brack gunman ramrod the outfit.

This morning, however, he was out on the range himself, working with a pair of Circle D riders to haze a small bunch of yearlings out of a rocky draw just west of Tinaja. Roundup operations had been rather tedious this year and the three men had worked some distance south of the usual range before locating the strays. It was Cotton Truesdale, a lantern-jawed redhead, who called Conree's attention to the rider who came swiftly toward them from the direction of Tinaja, a black figure looking even blacker as he rode hard out of the red sunrise.

"Somebody lookin' fer yuh, Jabe," Truesdale yelled above the clatter of moving cattle. "Looks like Brack's found hisself a new hand."

Conree shifted his squat body in the saddle to look, wary little eyes narrowed as he stared into the glare. Jabe didn't like new hands on his crew. Either they were gunmen thinly disguised as cowhands or they were likely to ask questions about the peculiar circumstances at Circle D. And Conree was not too good at concealing the things he knew had to be concealed. He would have liked his job a lot better if Brack had only been willing to run the cattle end of the business in a legitimate fashion and confine his fancy dealing to other lines.

Partly because Conree was resentful and partly because he was a good cattleman he looked back at his herd, ignoring the approaching stranger and giving his attention

26

to the task at hand. The other Circle D riders also had to pay attention to business as Conree sent the animals ahead of him a little too energetically. Consequently none of them saw the stranger when he changed his direction. All they knew was that he had swung to the south, keeping his bronc at a full gallop. He was still some three hundred yards away, but they could see him more clearly now as he moved out of the direct rays of the sun. A black clad man on a coal black horse.

"What d'yuh make o' that, Jabe?" Monty Howe called to the foreman. "Seems like that ranny changed his mind when he spotted us bustin' outa the draw. Plumb anxious to keep his distance, I'd say."

Conree stared at the black rider, then shrugged heavy shoulders in a gesture of dismissal and relief. Mexicans on the dodge were nothing new nor startling to him. What did it matter if a strange vaquero in holiday garb should take precautions against being challenged? Conree was glad enough that the man had not turned out to be another of Brack's disreputable recruits. Still he wondered why the fellow was heading back into the mountains where no one had lived since that young Wayne had been run out of the basin.

"Pick up them strays on the left," he bawled at Howe. "We're herdin' beef, not Mexs. 'Tend to business."

The black-clad rider chose a gulch some distance south of the one where Conree had picked up his yearlings, driving the black horse into it at the same headlong pace which he had been employing for the past mile. It was only when he was completely sheltered by the higher foothills that he relaxed and permitted his bronc to slow down.

"Kinda stuck our snoots into something then, black fella," he said aloud, apparently talking to the horse. It was a conversational sort of remark, partly relieved and partly rueful, but the noteworthy part of it was the accent. El Diablo Negro had completely lost his Latin tongue. The drawl had some of the usual Western flavor to it but there was something else as well, a certain shortening of vowels which contrasted with the broadness of the rest of it.

He did not speak again, but sent the horse through a narrow gulch whose rocky bottom would make tracking difficult. It had been no part of his plan to be seen in this part of the hills so he had to take due care as he worked his way into the higher foot-hills.

The trail led through a brief barren area and thence into a broad valley which lay behind the lower foothills of the Sierra Verdes. It was a pleasant valley, greener than the main expanse of the Javelina basin and insulated by the protecting fringe of rolling hills through which the black-clad rider had traveled. No mineral strike of any consequence had been made in this part of the country so the valley had been spared the upheavals which usually accompanied sudden wealth. It lay peacefully beneath the abrupt upsurge of the Sierra Verdes, its beauty the more notable because of the rocky heights which loomed on the west.

The stranger smiled a little as he saw the valley before him, the smile doing something to the lean face which had appeared so satanic with its black mustache and imperial. It was a smile in which satisfaction battled with something like grim anger, the conflict showing most notably in the hazel eyes. Pegleg Clancy would have been considerably interested if he had noticed those eyes. They were not the sort of eyes to be expected in a person of such swarthy skin.

The tall man swung the black bronc past a windowless log ranch house and a battered, broken-down corral. A precautionary survey told him that no one had come into the valley since his visit of the previous day, so he put the bronc into a clear flowing stream, entering the water at a long angle as though intending to follow the downstream course of the current. However, he did not continue in that direction any further than was necessary to lay the false trail. At a quiet word the black horse turned almost in his tracks and picked his way upstream, displaying a sure-footedness that would have done credit to a bighorn ram.

The stratagem was obvious enough and the black rider knew it. A good tracker would be certain to consider the possibility of such a move. He did not let the thought bother him, though; there had to be a beginning in any campaign and this was it. He kept to the brook for nearly a hundred yards, its course swinging in a wide arc which almost bounded the narrowing northern end of the valley. Then he found himself in a ravine where the scattered pines gave way to a cedar brake that was so dense as to form a complete tunnel over the brook. Beyond the cedar thicket he urged the black out of the water upon a rocky ledge where tracks would not show. The ledge in turn led to a stony glen where the cedars were equally thick, screening the glen so well that it might easily pass unnoticed. There the tall man dismounted and picketed the black horse before plunging afoot into the cedar brake.

He had to fight his way through the thicket but within a few seconds came out into the glen proper. It was a narrow slash in the mountain, overhung by one of the towering cliffs which marked the abrupt rise of the Sierra Verdes. No footholds were available on either side of the rocky wall nor was there any level ground immediately above it. Thus the glen was completely hidden from the view of anyone climbing upon the mountain above. The only entrance was the one through which the black rider had come. He knew it and let himself relax as he strode into the little opening. He even smiled a little at the scene behind the cedars, much as he had smiled at sight of the valley where the shattered ranch house was located. It was a smile in which several emotions battled for supremacy, real pleasure coming to the top for only a brief moment before losing ground to something sterner. Pegleg Clancy had not erred in thinking the black rider to be a man of bitter resolution.

The man's movements were brisk and efficient as he crossed to a crude but sturdy shack which had been built among the trees at the very base of the bluff. There he did a peculiar thing. Bringing out a hand mirror such as might have been an appurtenance to a lady's reticule he studied his own dark features with critical thoroughness. After that he exchanged the mirror for a length of rawhide rope and backed out of the hut.

A long-legged bay horse with four white fetlocks came out of the nearer woodland to meet him, showing signs of dubious interest. The man spoke gently, using the same peculiar drawl with which he had spoken to himself after avoiding the Circle D men. The intonation in some of the words was typically Southwestern, but here and there a vowel sound was slighted in a fashion which hinted at New England. It was an odd accent even for a country where tongues betray a dozen assorted backgrounds. Certainly it was not the precise Latin voice which had greeted Pegleg Clancy in Tinaja.

"Come on here, Cottonfoot, you ugly rascal," he called quietly to the bay pony. "I don't reckon you feel plumb sure about me in this outfit but I'm the real article. Come get yourself into the game. It's warmin' up fine." He chuckled without particular mirth and added, "Not that you're going to like the chore I've got lined up for you, but we'll make it short. I hope."

The big horse came forward a little more confidently, using the white feet in a mincing manner which hinted that the animal might be fast as well as big, powerful, unkempt and remarkably ugly. The man seemed to be seeing him just that way for he added still another comment as he reached out to stroke the bronc's nose. " 'With the mouth of a bell and a heart of Hell and the head of a gallows tree.' An English jasper wrote it that way, Cottonfoot. Seems like he almost must have had a good look at you."

He stroked the bay's shaggy neck for a moment or two, still talking in soothing tones as though trying to take away the sting of the insulting description. Then he led the bronc back through the thicket to where the black stallion was waiting. The contrast between the two ponies was a sharp one. Both were big, but there the resemblance ended. The black was graceful and perfectly groomed; the bay was just a big rugged horse with straggly white fetlocks and a coat that looked as though it had never known grooming. Only a smart horseman might have guessed that the bay was even faster than the racy-looking black.

The man paused long enough to efface all sign of his passage through the cedars, then he mounted the black and rode on down the rock ledge with the bay trotting along at the end of the lead rope. For a good five minutes he managed to stay on hard rock, following the base of the long cliff where his camp was so well concealed. Finally he sent the black into another mountain brook which led him to a winding, rocky trail which crossed the brook at a slightly lower elevation. It was not a well-defined trail but it was familiar enough to him, and he knew that it led directly into country where cattle had been grazing. That was quite an important factor; cattle tracks would help to make his own sign difficult to read.

An hour's easy ride into the north brought him out into lower foothills several miles away from the spot where he had avoided the Circle D men. He eased his way around a low, dome-shaped hill until he could see the ridges of the Circle D spread directly ahead of him. There he picketed both horses and went forward on foot to reconnoiter. He did not have to walk very far because he had known exactly where to dismount, having scouted the Circle D from this angle several times during the past week. From a break in the shoulder of the hill less than a hundred feet from his ponies, he could see the entire Brack establishment and at the same time keep himself quite out of sight.

His observations had told him that the ranch carried only a small staff in spite of its imposing proportions. The cattle crew didn't work out from here, but had a bunkhouse a couple of miles to the north. Usually there were only two employees here at Brack's headquarters, a handy man who did the odd jobs, and a burly female who seemed to be the housekeeper and cook. There was always the chance that there might be someone else on hand, so the watcher took his time about reaching any decision.

He uttered a half chuckle as he slipped into his chosen spot, getting quick satisfaction out of the sight of Jabe Conree heading north across a rise nearly half a mile away. Evidently Conree had left his roundup crew and had dropped in at the ranch house, but now he was leaving to return to his regular base of operations. With Brack certain to be in Tinaja at this hour of the day it seemed to leave the field reasonably clear.

Still the watcher scanned everything closely, making sure that he had overlooked nothing, before going back to his horses.

He again mounted the black, leaving the frowsy-looking bay to munch contentedly at the grassy hillside. After that he dropped all trace of concealment and rode boldly out into the open, striking directly for the showy log structure which had become the center of Chandler Brack's life as a cow country squire.

A man came out of the back door as he approached, a heavy-bodied man whose coarse black hair grew low over beetling brows. Beneath the brows a beak nose jutted in a long curve until the fellow resembled some sort of grotesque, hairy terrapin. The stranger remembered him well enough, had recognized him from afar while scouting the place. Turk had been a Brack employee even in the old days. No one seemed to know his real name but his tremendous nose had caused him to be tagged as "The Turkle." He had expressed violent displeasure with the title so many times, and with so much pain to the name-callers, that it had been shortened to Turk, a variation which seemed to please him quite well. As a cowhand he had been hopelessly incompetent but Chan Brack had kept him for his vicious fighting qualities, retiring him from actual range service only when Turk's slowness and stupidity had resulted in the nearly fatal injuries to Pegleg Clancy. For Chandler Brack's purposes Turk was a good man to have around, a dependable killer who would ask no questions.

Now the surly brute stared belligerently at the black rider, one heavy fist hooked into a broad leather belt in convenient proximity to the monster sheath knife which was carried there. Turk was not much of a gunman, although he could throw lead if he had to; mostly he preferred to use his enormously powerful hands, either as strangling devices or for wielding a knife. He let one of the thick fingers tap significantly against the knife handle as he held up the other paw in a warning gesture.

"Fur enough, greaser! What d'yuh want?"

The black rider halted, ignoring the insult and the open hostility. "The Senor Brack?" he inquired politely. "He is at home, no?" The Spanish accent was now in complete mastery over the Texas drawl and the Yankee twang.

"Naw. He ain't here."

"Eet ees too bad. I have mees heem, hey? Then I mus' spik weeth Senor Con-ree."

"Conree ain't here neither. What d'yuh wanta see him about?"

The rider seemed to hesitate. Then he spoke again, still in the same careful tones.

"There ees a message of some trouble from the Javelina country. I am to tell the Senor Brack. Eef I do not find heem I am to tell Senor Con-ree. Ees eet you are Senor Con-ree?"

Turk shook his head half angrily. "Hell, no!" he rumbled. "I told yuh Conree ain't here. Anyway I'm Brack's segundo around here. Jabe Conree's jest a dam' straw boss."

The stranger looked puzzled. At least he tried to. Actually he was enjoying a bit of grim amusement at the stupid gorilla's vanity. "I am meesenformed, perhaps," he said gently. "Eet ees most unfortunate."

The back door was flung open then and a huge, untidy woman crammed her body into the opening. "What was it ye wanted of Brack?" she demanded with harsh abruptness.

The visitor almost betrayed his astonishment. He had known that there was a woman in the Brack household but he had not even suspected that he might recognize her. Mamie Rook had been a plenty tough gal in her day, following the mining camps while she retained any vestige of youth or looks, and running various vicious deadfalls in frontier towns after weight and age took their toll. It was a bit of a shock to find that she had turned to cookery as a change from such gentle practices as rolling drunken miners.

"There ees a message for Senor Brack," the black rider told her with a formal bow. "From a man name of Dimmick at the Three Toes Mine. Eef I do not find Senor Brack I am to tell Senor Con-ree that he must take the message for heem."

"What kind of a message?" Mamie Rook demanded.

The black one shrugged. "Eat ees not to you, Senora, that I am to spik the words. You weel pardon, of course?"

"Rats! If Brack's got a message comin' to him we'll see that it gets delivered. Turk kin take it."

"Turk?"

"Him." She jerked a splayed thumb at the glowering chore man. "He's Brack's right-hand man, and I'm his missus. Ye kin pass the word on to us and we'll hand it to Brack."

The stranger seemed to consider the proposition at some length. Actually he was trying to recover from his second big surprise. So Turk was married to Mamie Rook! That was a hot one, even if the marriage was one of those informal affairs which were so common in this country.

"Veree well," he conceded finally. "Senor

Dimmick says there ees a new vein of pay ore showing. A good report, of course, but Senor Dimmick seemed to worry. He wanted that Senor Brack should have the word at once. Something beeg must be decided, I theenk."

Turk grunted something unintelligible, but Mamie snapped a quick exclamation. "It's that Moss deal, Turk. The one he was talkin' about to Conree this mornin'. He's figurin' to sell out the Three Toes to some Eastern dude before anybody finds out that the hole ain't producin' no more. Seems like I heard him say somethin' about meetin' this man Moss today."

"Yeah?" Turk commented vacantly. Evidently he was not getting the implications which were so clear to his more alert spouse.

The woman swung to face him, her words crisp and energetic as she tried to force the understanding into his dull wits. "Ye've got to git to him before he sells, honey. He won't like the idea if we let him sell out while it's still a good thing — and mebbe he'll be good for some nice change if we save him a bad mistake. Better high-tail it to Tinaja and pass the word so he kin sidetrack the sale 'til he finds out what's what."

"Why me?" Turk demanded. "Why can't

this greaser finish the chore he started?"

The man on the black stallion shrugged. "Pardon, Senor. I have finish. Already I lose time from my own affair. Thees morning I even mees breakfast to do the favor for Senor Brack. Eet ees enough."

Mamie nodded, curiosity and something else showing in her faded eyes. "Ye done all right, stranger," she conceded, ignoring Turk's scowl. "Come along in and I'll fix ye up a bite to eat. Turk kin take care o' things as soon as he gits the idea through his thick head."

Again there was a sullen rumble from the chore man, but Mamie cut him off sharply. "Shut up now, ye loon! Git a saddle on a hawss and make some fast tracks fer Tinaja. And git the message straight. Tell Brack it's from Dimmick. Pay dirt at the Three Toes. Don't sell yet. Got that?"

Turk nodded, still sullen.

"Sure? Say it over fer me. Go on now, say it!"

Turk did not look up but repeated the significant phrases in a low voice. Mamie nodded and waved him away with a huge red hand. "That's right. Now don't ferget it between here and Tinaja," she ordered. "Scoot!"

Turk did not even reply. He simply glared

at his wife and turned away, shambling off in the direction of the big stables. It was an exhibition which the black rider decided would be worth remembering. Mamie was boss over the stupid Turk, but the man was resentful of the fact. It might be a point worth keeping in mind.

"Come in and set," Mamie invited, suddenly affable. "I'd kinda like to hear all about it while I'm fixin' yuh up with a snack. Gold's always nice news to talk about."

If there was more in her glance than the words expressed, the messenger elected to ignore it. He dismounted and bowed again. "Pardon, Senora. My horse, I should take care of heem. A little water, perhaps, and a small bit of hay. Then I weel be most happy to accept your so kind eenveetation."

The fat woman frowned with impatience but managed to contort her big jowls into something which she seemed to feel was an expression of sweetness. "Right, brother," she agreed. "Help yerself at the stable. Nobody around to bother ye."

More useful information, the tall man thought as he led his horse away. Maybe he would have time to get a little more in the way of facts out of the fat woman before he had to get on with his big purpose of the day.

He made a long job of watering the black bronc, killing time at the water trough until Turk was out of sight on the trail to Tinaja. Then he led the black to a convenient hayrick and left him to feed. By that time he could feel a nervous tension coming over him. This was the hour he had been planning for, the moment of the real opening gun of his campaign. It wouldn't be an easy chore like tacking up old posters, either. There would be risk and trouble. The game was really being opened, and with heavy stakes riding on the success of the next couple of moves.

3

Tinaja had lost its early morning aura of peace when Chandler Brack rode his smartly groomed sorrel into town. Brack had once made a hobby of riding the fastest ponies available to him, but of recent months he had turned to big animals and showy ones. It was almost as though his mount was a part of his personality. A big horse helped to achieve the effect of dignity and importance, an end which had been Brack's ambition for more years than he liked to remember. Even when he had been running a land office on a shoestring he had made himself more than a little pompous, striving for a show of importance. Since his amazing turn of luck he had indulged his vanity a bit more openly. Gone was the shabby land agent with his poor pretenses, and in his place was Chandler Brack, owner of half of the Javelina basin, financial genius of Tinaja, mine owner, gentleman rancher and political boss of half the territory. There were men who might have hinted that these activities were not the sum total of the Brack interests but such hints were not healthy ones, and the potential hinters usually took good care to keep their thoughts secret.

Brack noted quickly that there was an unusual stir in town. Even though it was scarcely past breakfast time there were little knots of men standing around in front of saloons and stores, their idleness as conspicuous as their very presence. Oddly enough, all of the groups seemed ominously close to the Miners' Bank. For an instant Brack thought that the bank might have been robbed during the night but then he spotted the ungainly form of Abe Kline, Tinaja's town marshal, in one of the lounging groups. Evidently nothing serious had happened; Abe wasn't acting a bit excited or worried as he usually did at the first sign of trouble.

Still the gathering spelled uneasiness for Brack. He knew too many reasons why men might be ganging up like this to meet him. He reached stealthily around beneath the jaunty tails of the elegantly tailored frock coat, loosening his six gun in its holster. There was a nervous light in his black eyes as he made the move and the cleanly shaven, thick lips were drawn so tightly that they brought the bony jaw into unusual prominence. Chandler Brack might have a bad conscience, but he had his nerve with him every minute. It had taken plenty of sand to bring him along so far in a hard country and he didn't propose to give up for lack of that quality. If something had gone wrong with his crooked little empire he was just the man to fight matters to a deadly finish.

The first group of men in his path greeted him easily enough, and he relaxed almost as quickly as he had tensed himself. It was plain to be seen that the men of Tinaja were waiting for him but there had been no hostility in those first greetings, only a lively curiosity. That was enough to satisfy Brack. With any ordinary problem he felt sure that he would be able to make a satisfactory adjustment.

Then he spotted Boone Sabbath, a quiet little man whose unvarying gray suit almost made him look like a country parson. The clothing seemed to suit the mildness of his innocent blue eyes and the constant look of bewilderment on his pinched features. Many a greenhorn had been taken in by the appearance, but Sabbath had been a faro dealer in Tinaja long enough for men to

46

know something about him. They respected him mostly for his cold nerve, only a handful recognizing the carefully hidden fact that he was an important cog in Chandler Brack's growing organization.

Brack nodded carelessly as he approached the group where Sabbath stood. Boone ordinarily was not out of bed at such an early hour of the morning. This must be something special, all right.

"Morning, Boone," the big man said, smiling as he nodded his head in the direction of the various groups along the sidewalks. "Looks like everybody's up to see the circus train — or whatever it is."

Sabbath's little return nod was tacit recognition of his employer's request for information. "Tinaja had a visitor this morning, Mister Brack," he said quietly, almost formally. "A stranger rode into town just after dawn and posted a couple of notices offering rewards for the arrest of an outlaw known as El Diablo Negro." The mincing words fitted the little man's dapper appearance even as they were in sharp contrast to his known reputation. "Pegleg Clancy and Ben Arms saw the man who put up the signs and they think it was the outlaw himself."

Brack frowned, trying to make sense of

that final statement, but he offered no word of comment as he rode on toward the bank building. El Diablo Negro was not a new name to him, but he couldn't quite understand why the border outlaw should have come to Tinaja. Still he was ready to go into his act when Marshal Abe Kline stepped forward to repeat the information Sabbath had already passed along.

"El Diablo Negro, eh?" Brack repeated as the lanky marshal blurted out the main facts. "I thought the Texas Rangers had scared that two-bit bandit right out of the country." He laughed easily, winking at a couple of men who seemed most impressed by his offhand mirth.

"That ain't what I heard," Kline countered, pulling nervously at an enormous ear which by its very size added to the narrowness of his brown face. "I heard the jigger was dead. That was the report a couple o' years ago. Now it looks like he's up to his monkey tricks again. Both Ben Arms and Pegleg Clancy seen him put up the signs and they figure it was Diablo. 'Specially Ben. He knows the feller from over Texas way."

"Any idea why he's posting signs against himself?" Brack asked, still without any great show of interest.

"Nope. They ain't even new signs. They been used before. That's kinda why we're all waitin' around for yuh to arrive."

"Huh?" This time Brack let his surprise show. "Why?"

" 'Cause Clancy says the outlaw shoved an extry poster under the bank door. Everybody's curious to see what it's like."

Brack grunted again, the sound indicating a mixture of surprise and annoyance. It was not comforting to realize that he had been singled out for the mysterious attentions of a locoed bandit. Still it did not seem like a very serious matter, and he smiled again as he urged the sorrel forward toward the sturdy little brick building. "We'll look it over, Abe," he promised.

His movements, however, made it clear that the words had been no invitation. He pushed through the crowd with scant ceremony, leaving Abe Kline behind him. At the door he turned the bronc over to gray old Columbus Alsop, the bank clerk who had to do extra duty as wrangler each morning. That was another well-known part of the Brack routine. He always made Lum Alsop stable the horse, and he had two good reasons for insisting on the chore. In the first place the menial duty kept the old man from getting above himself, or so Brack figured, and in the second place it permitted Brack to enter the bank without any immediate observer. There was no point in taking the unnecessary risk of having someone else watch the safe opening process. Chandler Brack trusted no one — largely because he knew that no one should ever trust Chandler Brack.

He unlocked the heavy oak door, his back to the surging crowd, and slipped through into the bank without permitting anyone to follow him. With one swift move he banged the door in the faces of the bolder citizens, then stooped to pick up the rectangle of soiled cardboard which lay at his feet.

For a moment he stared in perplexity. This was in no way unusual, merely the conventional poster advertising for the arrest of a known criminal. Actually it was a duplicate of the one which was posted in front of the Gem, but Brack could not know that. He studied the description carefully for a few minutes without learning anything of interest, then turned the poster over in his heavy fingers as he strode back toward the rear room which served him as a private office. Instantly his curiosity changed to something much less impersonal. On the back of the placard was a message in heavily drawn capital letters, letters which had been made with the kind of marking crayon commonly used by express companies for marking crates and boxes. The message was concise and unpleasantly meaningful.

"EL DIABLO NEGRO RIGHTS WRONGS. HE KNOWS WHO KILLED JOSHUA LLOYD. THIS IS THE FIRST WARNING."

Chandler Brack swore violently from deep in his heavy throat. Then he went on into the office, avoiding the glances of the men whose outlines were showing at the barred windows of the bank building. He needed time to think, time to decide what this sinister message really meant. It was all right to laugh off the performance of the notorious Diablo as something exaggerated in the telling, but this was no laughing matter now. Until this very moment there had never been even a whisper of doubt expressed about the murder of Josh Lloyd. Everyone seemed to accept the law's verdict that had made Perry Wayne the guilty party, especially when Wayne made his break from the calaboose and disappeared. It had been a closed incident — happily closed so far as Chan Brack was concerned. Now a crazy Mexican outlaw was threatening to open the whole matter, hinting that he knew the

51

real truth. Obviously this was going to take some careful handling.

The moment of near panic passed quickly. Brack had known other spots of sharp crisis in his rapid rise to wealth, and he did not propose to let himself get foolish now. Certainly he had to keep this threat a secret until he could find some means of getting rid of Diablo. And the entire male population of Tinaja was crowding around the bank to learn about the poster!

"Easy enough," he said aloud, some of the old confidence showing in the words. "If they want to see the poster I'll show it to the damned fools."

It was a simple matter after all. A few tacks from a desk drawer and within a half minute the poster was prominently displayed on the wall just beyond the little wicket where Lum Alsop would be handling the ordinary affairs of banking. Now everyone could see and no one would even suspect that there was a threat on the back of the paper. Brack even chuckled a little as he went to the safe and opened it. He was still chuckling in fine good humor when he opened the door and permitted his old clerk to enter upon his duties of setting the bank up for the day's business. It was almost funny to see the disappointment on men's faces when they discovered that the poster on the bank wall was just like one of the others.

Brack spent a few minutes with the curiosity seekers, gossiping idly over the morning's mystery and making light of the whole fantastic business. Then he slipped back into the private office and closed the door. Now that he had displayed the proper nonchalance it was time for him to do some thinking.

One conclusion came without very much arduous thought. Perry Wayne must have something to do with this attack. No one except Wayne could have had an inkling of the real truth about Lloyd's death, so it must be Wayne's information that was back of Diablo's message. Maybe Wayne had actually employed the Mexican as a gesture of revenge. In either event the answer would have to be the same. Diablo had to be eliminated. If Wayne was an active participant in the game there would have to be a double killing.

Brack considered the possibilities for the better part of an hour, trying to imagine what had happened in the two year interval since the arrest and subsequent escape of Perry Wayne. Obviously the young man had become a fugitive, and the fact had thrown him into the company of El Diablo Negro.

From Brack's point of view there were good features in that as well as bad ones.

Presently he shrugged his heavy shoulders and helped himself to a stiff drink from the bottle which always rested in the bottom compartment of the big desk. Brack was too smart a man to do much drinking, and he usually avoided the bottle entirely at this hour of the day, but now he felt the need of the stimulant. Not that he would have admitted any trace of nervousness but he still felt the need of a drink.

He went out then, greeting passers-by with the careful geniality which had become such a constant part of his pose. He liked to play the role of the benevolent overlord to these Tinaja citizens, and he handled the part so well that few of them ever came to resent it.

To all intents and purposes his morning walk was an aimless one but presently he turned in at the Palo Duro. No one was in the bar at that hour, and Brack glanced around carelessly, passing a casual comment to the apron before passing through to an inner hallway which led to the stairs. No one met him along the way, and his climb to the upper story was likewise without witnesses.

From his pocket he drew a key, letting

himself into a rear room which overlooked a stable and a remarkably untidy back yard. It was the apartment he customarily occupied when business or weather conditions prevented him from traveling back and forth to the big ranch in the foothills. Tinaja understood that Brack was owner of the Palo Duro, but few people even suspected the remarkable meetings which took place in this room.

He sat down quietly, listening until a cautious footfall beyond the door told him that he had a visitor. Boone Sabbath came in with scarcely a sound, his parsonlike calm making him seem like a sorrowful clergyman arriving at a deathbed. "You wanted me, I suppose, Chan," he stated, almost in a whisper.

It didn't sound like a question, but Brack replied, "Sure."

"About that third poster?"

"How did you know?"

"I figured. It wasn't slipped under your door for nothing."

"You could have known it some other way." Brack's harsh voice didn't increase in volume, but the menace in it was not lost on the gambler.

"I could? Maybe you ought to explain that, Chan."

"I mean the paper hinted at something which nobody knows but the two of us."

"Better explain it all. I'm not much good at riddles."

"All right. There was a note on the back of that paper, a note to the effect that our friend Diablo knows who killed Josh Lloyd. Not many men have the information that would let them pass such a hint."

Sabbath took a chair, his lips forming a soundless whistle until he brought out a cheroot and lighted it with calm deliberation. Then he blew out a cloud of smoke and stared straight at Brack. "I see your point, Chan. And I'm telling you now that I don't know a thing about it. Your secret has been plenty safe with me."

Brack studied him at some length, the heavy features grim and forbidding. "I think I believe you, Boone," he said finally. "Heaven help you if I ever find myself changing my mind."

"Keep your head and you won't have any reason to change your mind," Sabbath retorted, still completely calm. "Now let's take it from there. I didn't spill the story. You didn't. Who did?"

Brack lifted heavy shoulders in a gesture of defeat but answered the question immediately. "Wayne, of course. The young fool must have finally used his head."

Sabbath puffed steadily at the cigar, then removed it from tight lips to stare reflectively at the cone of white ash. "Could be," he conceded. "Then you figure he hired the Mex to stir things up?"

"What else?"

"What's he trying to do?"

"Your guess is as good as mine. I'm guessing he's after revenge. Or maybe he hopes he can shake me down for hush money. He probably knows I've come up in the world so he thinks I'm ripe for a shakedown. In a day or two I ought to get his demands."

Sabbath's eyes narrowed a little. "And then?" he asked, his voice dropping just a shade.

"What do you think?"

The gambler's thin face cracked just a little then, something almost like a smile showing on it. "I think we play up to him long enough to locate him. And to get a good line on the Mex. Then — bang!"

"Bang!" Brack agreed grimly. "That's all. Keep your eyes open around town."

As the faro dealer started for the door, Brack added, "Send Abe up. On the quiet, of course."

"Right." The door closed behind Sabbath, and Brack crossed to the room's only window, staring out at the rugged outlines of the Sierra Verdes. In the stable yard below him a little warped-bodied man moved about slowly, sometimes casting an eye toward the window of Brack's room, but the big man paid no attention. He was thinking in terms of his own plans, beginning to boast a little in his own mind. So they thought they'd scare Chan Brack, did they? Somebody was about due to learn a lesson — a lesson which would do the learner no good at all.

He turned from the window only as another footstep sounded from the hall. A fist knocked guardedly at the door and the big man asked, "Abe? That you?"

"Yep."

"Come in. It's unlocked."

The lanky town marshal slid in awkwardly but without sound. He was definitely not a handsome man, his long face almost as narrow as the tiny features of Boone Sabbath. Where Sabbath was alert and sharp, though, Abe Kline was simply ugly and lean. He pulled again at one of the outflung ears, watching Brack with an unspoken question in his eyes.

"Got a job for you," Brack said. "That Diablo jigger is up to some kind of hell. I want him fixed for keeps."

Kline frowned. "The reward poster wants him alive," he protested.

"Don't be a damned fool, Abe! Those posters are five or six years old. They don't mean a thing."

"Then what's the idee?"

"Listen." Brack was concealing his impatience with an effort. "Diablo wants to call attention to himself. Don't ask me why, but believe me. So he put up the signs. That got him all the attention he wanted. And it can't hurt him a bit because nobody wants him anywhere nowadays. Just take my word for it that the posters are a ruse — and the only way to break up whatever crooked game he's playing is to get rid of him. The sooner Diablo gets to be a corpse the sooner I'll be ready to hand out some bonus money to anybody who takes care of the chore."

Kline pulled again at one of the big ears. He was evidently puzzled, but he knew better than to ask too many questions of the man who had put him into office — and who could get him out again if he wanted to. "Gotcha, boss," he agreed. "Any idee where the sidewinder's apt to be holed up?"

"No. But I imagine he'll show himself again before long. That business of posting signs wasn't done for nothing; he wants folks to recognize him when he makes his next play. So you get ready, and don't miss. Maybe I'm not sure just what his game is, but I'll be willing to do my own guessing if you fix it so he'll never be able to tell me. In fact, you'd better make sure that it happens that way."

"Gotcha, boss," Kline said again. "Anything else?"

"No. Just keep your eyes open and your mouth shut. Fog him down when you spot him. With his reputation you don't need any extra reason."

"Gotcha, boss."

Chandler Brack's spirits had reached almost a peak of optimism when he let himself out of the room and sauntered back down the stairs to the first floor of the Palo Duro. It was a mighty convenient thing to have lieutenants available, men who would do his bidding without asking too many questions. Tinaja didn't need to know that he had issued any orders to either Sabbath or Kline but the work would be handled neatly, he knew. Both men had performed with efficiency on other occasions.

He fairly exuded confidence and prosperity as he strolled back to the bank, putting on his best act as the benevolent patron of everything in Tinaja. The act was partly intended to lull any suspicions which might linger in the minds of men who thought about that third poster; partly it was just a normal pose. Chan Brack had become a big man in the Javelina basin, and he didn't want anyone to forget it.

He was still handing out cordial greetings to everyone when he passed through the main room of the bank and entered his private office. The stage from Oro City had arrived during his absence and there was mail on his desk. He decided to take care of the mail before turning his thoughts to the real problem which he had planned for today's subject — a problem which the Diablo matter had almost driven from his thoughts.

Most of the correspondence was routine and he went through it swiftly, pausing with a perplexed frown only when he came to a tiny package bearing an Oro City postmark. It was addressed to Chandler Brack, Miners' Bank, Tinaja, and it was just about the right size to contain a watch or a piece of jewelry.

He grunted aloud as he reached for a knife and cut the sturdy cord which held the brown wrapper in place. What could this be?

Inside the wrapper was a plain cardboard box, and inside the box was a tube of more wrapping paper. Brack grunted again, unrolling the paper a little angrily until he found himself holding an empty, tarnished brass cartridge case. For a moment he saw nothing unusual about the case or the package, but then his eye caught a glimpse of the lettering which lined the roll of brown paper. It was black lettering, in bold capitals, almost certainly done with the same crayon that had printed the message on the back of the reward poster.

"IF YOU DO NOT BELIEVE EL DIABLO NEGRO KNOWS THE TRUTH, THIS WILL CONVINCE YOU. FIFTY-EIGHT CALIBER SHELLS ARE NOT SO COMMON THAT YOU WILL HAVE FORGOTTEN. NO OTHER WARNING WILL BE GIVEN."

The big man sat back for a long time, staring from the cartridge case to the message and back to the case again. A few minutes earlier he had been guessing; now he knew. It had seemed likely that Perry Wayne would be back of this crazy Diablo business; now it was a certainty. A fifty-eight caliber shell had been the crowning piece of evidence in the case against young Wayne, a fact which the framed man would certainly have remembered with bitterness.

For a minute or two Brack was in a complete state of fury. He considered going out into town to amend his orders to Kline and Sabbath, but then he controlled himself sternly. This was no time to get foolish. He had to keep his head — because this whole game was probably an attempt to scare him and he couldn't afford to play into the enemy's hands. Kline and Sabbath had their orders. There was nothing more to be done just now. The cartridge could be treated just like the third poster. It was a bit of evidence to be concealed until such time as the whole matter could be closed out. Brack's lips tightened into a wolfish grin as he let the final phrase repeat itself in his mind. A smart man always had a way of handling troublemakers.

4

The black-clad stranger knocked once at the circle D back door, stepping into the kitchen at Mamie's shout of invitation. The fat woman was at the stove, and there was a good breakfast waiting.

"Better take on some chuck, honey," the big woman greeted, offering what she seemed to think was a coy smile as she nodded toward the food. "Then we kin have a real good talk, you and me. I'm kinda curious about the Three Toes, ye might say. I'd ha' swore it was all petered out."

There was something comically disgusting about her in the way she combined greediness, vanity and a repulsive appearance. The stranger nodded, not trusting himself to speak again at that point, and started across the room as though to avail himself of the hospitality. He changed his tactics abruptly as he passed behind Mamie. It was clear that she was backing deliberately into his path, but the result was certainly not what she had expected. He put a hard arm around her neck, squeezing tight against her windpipe as he used his other hand to grab her right wrist and bend it up and back in a relentless hammerlock.

"Sorree to be unpleasant to so fine a lady," he hissed, overdoing the irony just a little. "The food I appreciate but thees must be done. You weel pardon, I am sure."

There was a smothered curse as the big woman struggled helplessly in the bend of that smothering arm. Then she was thrown to the floor while the intruder made swift, deft motions, releasing the stranglehold as he lashed fat wrists behind the broad back. Mamie swore loudly but helplessly as the strings of her own apron became her bonds. The stranger added to the security of his package by tying her feet together with heavy cord from a drawer of the kitchen cupboard, completing the job with a gag made from a slightly soapy dishrag. Then he stooped to get a firm hold under the woman's shoulders.

"Again I regret, Senora," he murmured politely. "Eet weel be but a brief time."

He dragged her into a deep pantry closet and threw another lashing or two from her wrists to shelf brackets on either side. "Be quiet," he advised, "and you weel be comfortable. Struggle and you weel find the lashing veree tight. Adios, Senora."

He even permitted himself a very correct little bow as he backed out of the pantry. His words, however, were scarcely gallant as he muttered, "Good thing my grandfather was a whaleman. Handling blubber runs in the family." He made certain that the woman could not hear that use of his normal accent.

He closed the door behind him then and was about to turn toward the front of the building when he was interrupted by an order that was none the less startling for the obvious nervousness in the speaker's voice.

"Put up your hands, you bandit, or I'll — I'll shoot!" It was a woman's voice, and the tremble in it seemed to come from anger as well as from nervousness.

The tall man knew a flash of irritation at himself that he should have been so careless. His daily observations had told him that Mamie and Turk were the only regular residents of the Circle D ranch house, and they had practically admitted as much in their talk, but it had still been foolish to make any rash assumptions. On this job a man couldn't afford even one mistake.

He kept his voice calm, however, speaking

in the same precise tones as he turned and shoved his lean hands to shoulder height. "The honor is all mine, Senorita. I deed not know Senor Brack was so happy as to have such fine company."

The comment was partly a matter of playing the ironically polite Latin, partly an expression of the swift thought which passed through his mind. Chan Brack's murky past had been quite lurid with female complications, and the intruder knew that he should have been alert to the possibility of something like this. Just because Mamie had been the only woman around Circle D in the past week was no reason to assume that none would appear.

Along with the practical thought he realized that he was looking at a most attractive young woman. Chan Brack had indeed picked himself a winner this time. The girl was rather tall but so perfectly proportioned that she gave no particular impression of height. Her blonde hair was a shade darker than honey, setting off an oval face that would have been pretty if she had not been squinting so sternly along the barrel of a well-polished forty-four. Even with the determined squint there was something interesting in her blue eyes. Neither anger nor fear could quite dispel the hint of humor there, and the tall man knew a sense of regret that such a woman could have thrown herself away on Chandler Brack. He forced the thought away promptly, however. No one with a Brack label was worthy of any moment of pity or sympathy. Probably this girl wouldn't appreciate it anyway.

"What are you trying to do?" she demanded, her voice steadying a little.

The tall man forced a smile. After the first shock of dismay at his own error he had found time to make an interesting observation. This girl might be a tough citizen, but she didn't know much about guns. She was trying to act ominous while aiming an uncocked single-action revolver at him.

"Does eet matter?" he asked, stepping forward quietly. The gap between them closed as he spoke, and before she could realize her danger he took the extra couple of strides that brought him within reach of the gun.

There was no question as to the deadliness of her intentions. She squeezed hard on the trigger without any result and he pinned her with one arm while he took the gun away with his free hand. "The holdup lady should always cock the gun," he murmured, still keeping his voice low. "Eet shoots so much better that way."

She tried to wrench herself away, fighting silently instead of screaming. For a moment he found himself with quite a battle on his hands, particularly because he had to make sure that she did not ruin his disguise. It meant keeping himself at her back so he tossed the gun into a far corner and used both hands. Again she displayed prompt good sense, ceasing her struggles when it became clear that she could not hope to break away.

"The lady ees smart," he commended, his voice almost a whisper in her ear. "One wonders that so smart a senorita throws herself away on that peeg of a Brack. Mamie I could understand but —"

She twisted in his grasp, freeing a hand to slap him hard across the cheek. The anger in her blue eyes made him wonder a little. Almost it seemed that she had been more angry at the taunt than at the rest of the affair.

There was no time to think about such matters, however. He subdued her once more and shoved her ahead of him into a room which he decided would be Chan Brack's private quarters. It was a room on which much money had been spent, but he did not have time to admire its sumptuous furnishings. He held the girl firmly, using a couple of Brack's fanciest cravats to bind her wrists and elbows. Then he tripped her and threw her face down on the tumbled bed while he used still another cravat to lash the trim ankles together.

"Again eet ees a regret," he told her softly. "Today I am mos' unpolite to the ladies. There will be no good een shouting so I omit the gag."

He went out and shut the door behind him. A swift glance from a doorway satisfied him that no one was approaching the house so he sat down and made a swift job of the meal which his sadly mistreated hostess had supplied for him. After that he went out into the back yard and mounted the black horse, swinging the animal quickly toward the spot where he had left the bay. There he picked up the extra bronc's lead rope and turned back toward the ranch house.

He tied both horses at the kitchen door and went into the house again, checking briefly to see that the snorting Mamie and the coldly furious blonde girl were both secure. After that his movements had a sparkle in them that hinted at grim pleasure. Even with the great danger under which he was working it was good fun to despoil the enemy in this fashion, not only because it represented a definite move in the campaign of nerves, but also because it would strike Brack in the spots where he was most easily hurt, his greed and his pride. In substance that was the real goal of the program anyway. Brack had to be angered and confused or there would be no hope of baiting him into the false move that would be essential to any real success.

Working swiftly, the raider supplied himself with a quantity of food, principally canned goods and other packaged articles. In the event of a long war he wanted supplies that would keep in the mountain hideout where they would have to be stored. In spite of his haste he made careful choices, wrapping the plunder into two bundles contrived from blankets rummaged out of a closet in Brack's room. They were fine quality blankets, he noticed, even as he bowed ironically to the girl who stared at him in angry silence. He did not speak to her, however, merely taking the blankets and going out into the kitchen to make up his packs. When everything was ready he carried them to the back door and lashed them across the back of the bay pony, balancing the load as well as possible.

"Not a very good pack, Cottonfoot," he told the horse whimsically, "but I kinda warned you about it. Anyway, you won't have to tote it so very far, so try to keep your dignity under control for a little while." Once more the Latin intonation was conspicuously absent while the odd combination of twang and drawl was back again. He patted the outraged bronc a couple of times and went briskly back into the house.

This time the plundering expedition was short and to the point. From a gunrack in the massive and ornate living room he selected a new Winchester rifle, examining its action swiftly before laying it aside and digging into a drawer for two packages of cartridges to fit it. "Right nice rifles Brack buys," he muttered to himself. "In fact, a right nice place all around, includin' the female company. Took a heap o' crooked money to buy all this."

The words expressed a feeling which he had been repressing ever since entering the building. Chandler Brack had made a show place of his ranch house, sparing no expense to make it worthy of the man who owned a bank, a mine, half a town and most of a valley. The house was low, solidly built and spacious, its rooms seeming huge with their paneled ceilings against log walls which had been finished inside to show a satiny polish. Brack had indeed fitted himself out like the feudal lord he considered himself. With so much wealth back of him he was going to be a mighty hard man to beat.

The plunderer forced the thought from his mind. There was no point in dwelling upon his own bitterness. That was not the way to fight an efficient campaign. A man had to keep his head. Bitterness might have been a major factor in driving him into this fantastic attempt at justice, but now that the game was under way emotions had to be kept under control. Better to ignore the enemy's ill-gotten magnificence and stick to business. Nobody would ever hurt Chan Brack just by hating him.

Carrying the rifle and cartridges he crossed to another door and glanced into the room, more out of curiosity than anything else. Somewhat to his surprise it was another bedroom, evidently a well-appointed guest room, judging by the impersonal nature of its expensive furnishings. There was nothing impersonal about the feminine garments in the room, though. Evidently this had become the quarters of the mysterious blonde who had so nearly upset a lot of fine calculations.

The tall man frowned, wondering whether he had misjudged the girl. Maybe she wasn't what he had thought. He turned on his heel, striding swiftly into the room where he had left her. "Again my apologies," he said, letting the sibilance of the border come back into his tones. "Maybe you are not comfortable here?"

She glared wordlessly at him, and he dumped his burden on the foot of the bed to lift her bodily and carry her across to the other bedroom. She maintained a stony silence and he left her without further words on his part. If he had been wrong about her this would relieve her embarrassment a little; if he had been right it wouldn't make any difference.

Then he put her out of his thoughts completely as he went back to survey the expensive interior of Brack's room. There was a huge bureau across one of the far corners, its broad mirror looming so large that it seemed to double the already vast proportions of the apartment. It must have cost a pretty piece of dinero to freight that bit of furniture out here into the foothills, but now that it was here it offered an excellent target for the next salvo.

He drew from his shirt pocket a heavy black marking crayon and proceeded to print a message in bold capitals upon the spotless surface of the mirror.

"EL DIABLO NEGRO WOULD THANK

YOU FOR THE SUPPLIES YOU HAVE PROVIDED ONLY THEY DID NOT BELONG TO YOU BY RIGHT. THEY WERE BOUGHT WITH BLOOD MONEY. DIABLO TAKES THEM AS HIS OWN. TODAY YOU LOSE FOOD AND AMMUNITION. TOMORROW YOU LOSE REPUTATION. AFTER THAT QUIEN SABE? THE TRUTH DOES MIRACLES. LLOYD WILL BE AVENGED."

He had to crowd his letters a little at the bottom to get it all on, but presently he stood back to scowl wryly at the finished job.

"Very juvenile," he said, half aloud. "Sounds like something I might have written in the sixth grade. But maybe it's just as well. Brack can't expect any great degree of literary merit in a warning note chalked on a mirror by a border bandit."

There was one other matter to be taken care of, and the tall man did it deliberately and thoughtfully, the sardonic smile gone from his lips as he worked. He placed a single brass shell case on the bureau in front of the printed message. It was an exploded shell such as might have been picked up almost anywhere, but he knew that it would have a special meaning for Chandler Brack.

It was fifty-eight caliber, like another one which had been placed in the mail. They ought to give the rascally banker something to think about.

"I just hope they'll soften him up for further treatment," he grumbled to himself as he turned to leave the room. This time he went out without further delay, not even looking around when he heard the sounds of Mamie's grunts from the pantry. Five minutes later he was out of sight of the house, moving easily through the foothills of the Sierra Verdes with the loaded bay pony ambling discontentedly along behind him.

He returned to the hidden glen by the same route he had used in leaving it, taking no particular precautions against trackers until he left the dim trail and climbed through the brook to the complicated pattern of rock ledges. There he moved slowly and with painstaking care, keeping an alert eye behind him to see that the bay did not stray from the narrow line of rocks and leave any sort of betraying sign. It took still more time to get the loaded bronc through the cedar thicket, but finally he had his entire outfit within the confines of the protecting brake. After that he went back to do a meticulous job of trail blotting at the spot where he had entered the cedars. Even then he did not relax. There was still much work to be done, and it was only a question of time until the hills would be swarming with outraged manhunters goaded on by the desperation of Chandler Brack.

The stolen supplies were cached in the shack, the black horse was unsaddled, and both ponies were given a brisk rub-down. Then the tall man crossed again to the shack and began to take off the black garb which had made him so conspicuous to such a variety of people during the morning. Each garment was dusted carefully and folded before being wrapped in a poncho. Maybe he would never need them again, but it would be well to keep the whole outfit in good condition in case of some unexpected emergency.

In place of the ornate black garb he put on torn Levi's, a faded brown flannel shirt, well-scuffed Texas boots, and a cheap vest that was a little too large for him. A loose red bandana around his neck and a huge but disreputable Stetson on his head would complete the outfit, but he donned neither of these yet. Instead he got a panful of water from the rill which edged the sheer cliff and went to work on his face and neck.

Careful scrubbing relieved him of most of

the swarthiness, leaving only a normal outdoor tan. Then he brought out scissors and a razor to remove the mustache, goatee and sideburns. In a matter of minutes the satanic features of El Diablo Negro had disappeared, leaving in their stead the face of a young fellow of pleasant enough appearance. Only the black hair remained and the young man surveyed it a little wryly in the mirror which was part of his kit.

"Good thing that hair dye is fast stuff," he remarked, half aloud. "It's all I've got left to keep me from being Perry Wayne again."

He wrinkled his upper lip tentatively, aware of a bare feeling now that the carefully cultivated mustache was gone. A second look into the mirror warned him that he would have to be careful about the lip and chin. The skin was not so evenly tanned where the facial ornaments had shaded it. So he smudged the clean shaven face judiciously before putting away the shaving tools. Nothing could be left to chance at this stage of the game; his next role was going to be even harder to play than the El Diablo Negro part.

Finally he turned away to where the broncs were cropping the lush grass of the little glen. "I reckon we pulled it off so far, pards," he said aloud, exaggerating his drawl

78

a little. "At least two men in Tinaja saw me, and Jabe Conree's boys will pass the word along. Not that I'm goin' to need extra publicity when Mamie Rook starts spoutin' off. El Diablo Negro is goin' to be a plumb famous outlaw in this basin." He chuckled with just a shade of the bitterness underlying the mirth. He wasn't fooling himself with the mild boast. There might have been a certain amount of rough humor in the act he had just put on, but he was fully aware of the dangerous nature of the entire scheme. He was undertaking a dangerous game, one where the stakes were his life against the wealth and power of an unscrupulous man — a game in which the opponent held every high card.

"With bullets the only wild card," he muttered. "Kind of a bad spot fer a young feller."

The whimsy helped him to relax then, and he spent some time checking plans and equipment with due care before hauling an extra saddle out of the little hut. It was everything that the black pony's ornate saddle had not been. It was old, stained, and generally dilapidated, but a sharp observer might have noted that there were no unrepaired breaks in important places. The cinches were strong and the latigo straps hid their newness under shrewdly applied stains. The tapideros were Army discards, but they had been repaired with a clumsiness that hid their serviceability. It was the outfit of a grub line rider, just as the clothing he now wore was the garb of a cowpoke down on his luck. Maybe it would be an efficient disguise; Wayne could only hope so.

He threw the battered old hull on the bay, talking in low tones to the animal as he did so. It was funny the way a man felt about a horse, he reflected. It always seemed so natural to talk to the jugheaded rascal, but he never seemed to offer his real confidences to the black. Even though the black was just as good a horse, perhaps even smarter and certainly more of a picture horse. Maybe it was just as well. The black had been part of a difficult disguise, and it wouldn't have been good policy to get into the habit of holding drawling confabs while posing as a Mexican. A man couldn't forget himself even for an instant in this show.

He left the glen as carefully as he had entered it, taking the same careful pains to blot out his back trail at the strategic point where he had emerged from the cedars. Then he retraced his early route, the one he had used in coming in from the lower valley. He kept the bay in the brook north of the battered ranch house until he spotted the trail where he had ridden the black into the water. Passing the spot by a matter of a few yards he let the pony climb to dry ground. Now anyone trailing the black in from the open country toward Tinaja might pick up the new trail by mistake. A big horse had gone into the stream and a big horse had come out. Only a remarkable tracker would be able to spot any difference in the two trails. Careful shoeing had prepared him for just such a stratagem. Now he could circle out of the valley and feel pretty sure that anyone trailing El Diablo Negro from Tinaja would be led straight back toward the town. Maybe it wouldn't be more than a minor puzzle to the men Brack would soon have on the trail, but it was better than letting them start on any thorough search of the hills. He had to play every card for what it was worth.

5

Pegleg Clancy had put in an uneasy morning. In a way it was pleasant to be a part of a continuing community excitement, but he was not ready to let himself be caught up in the flurry of pleased interest which had swept the town. Tinaja might be having a lot of fun out of an unaccustomed bit of spectacular gossip, but Pegleg had his own thoughts and he preferred to keep them to himself.

Anyway, it was Ben Arms who was getting the real attention. It had been Arms who had done the talking, explaining the posters to early rising citizens and improving his yarn each time he told it until finally he was making quite a story of it. He gave the impression that he had witnessed a most spectacular show, and he described El Diablo Negro in minute detail — in spite of the fact that he had seen only the man's back and at a considerable distance.

Clancy was content to have it that way. Arms could do the talking; Clancy would keep his mouth shut and his eyes open, hoping to see some sort of reaction that would explain the odd performance of the black rider. For Clancy was certain that an explanation should be coming up quickly.

The watching had been interesting enough, even though the little man had seen nothing of a really enlightening nature. At first there had been the wave of excitement as men gathered to study the signs on the express company door and in front of the Gem. To Clancy that part had been unimportant; what he wanted to see was that third placard in the bank. He had been one of the most interested members of the crowd in the street when Brack rode into Tinaja, and his disappointment had been keen when it was discovered that the poster was like the others.

Still Clancy was not satisfied. There had been something mighty peculiar about Brack's attitude when he first went into the bank, something which hinted at apprehension. Clancy wondered what had happened to make the man so calm just a few minutes later. The curiosity in his mind was great enough to keep him on the street after that, in spite of the fact that he usually turned in for some sleep after taking care of the opening chores at the Palo Duro. He didn't know what he hoped to learn, but he spent quite a bit of time in listening to the gossip that was running riot in town.

There were plenty of men in Tinaja who claimed to know something about the Robin Hood of the Rio Grande. Most of them admitted that their knowledge was purely hearsay, but a few claimed to have seen the outlaw at one time or another. Oddly enough, most of them seemed to feel that there had been a definite report of Diablo's death, that he had been shot by one of his own men. No one could pin the story down, however, and it soon was ignored in the excitement of speculation. How could Diablo have been killed when he was back in business? And what was he doing that he should want to advertise himself in this suicidal fashion? Clancy was interested to note that no one was offering much in the way of answers.

His greater interest was not in the crowd, though, but in the actions of Chandler Brack. At first the man had seemed thoroughly worried. Then he had disappeared for a few minutes with the third poster and had turned up again with all of his old confidence, placing the poster on the bank wall for all to see. It almost fooled Clancy — but not quite. He posted himself where he could keep an eye on the bank and was soon rewarded by sight of Brack coming out on the street. From that point Clancy could call every move with some exactness. He hadn't been working around the Palo Duro all these weeks without realizing that the hotel was the real meeting place for Brack's top hole lieutenants.

Consequently he went around into the back yard, showing himself negligently in the open before climbing to the loft of the stable and taking up his position at a peephole from which he could get a good view of Brack's private room. He couldn't hear any of the talk, of course, but he saw enough to make him mighty certain that something was afoot. Brack had issued orders to both Sabbath and Kline — and Clancy would have offered good odds on the nature of those orders.

He was back on the street in time to witness Brack's return to the bank. Five minutes later there was a new development. Monty Howe, one of the few Circle D riders who actually worked at the cattle business, loped into town with a couple of errands to perform for the outfit. He reported seeing a black-clad stranger at the edge of the Sierra Verdes, a furtive rider who had appeared anxious to avoid contact with the Circle D.

That was enough to stir up a new wave of interest. It ruined one of the best features of the Ben Arms story, though. No longer could Ben linger over the intriguing way Diablo had seemed to disappear into thin air. Now everyone knew that the mystery rider had cut west into the Sierra Verdes. That fact and the talk about the stagecoach passengers could provide plenty of gossip for the balance of the morning.

Clancy paid little attention to the other matter, but he soon understood that two Easterners had arrived on the morning stage from Oro City. One was a small man in well-tailored tweeds, while the other was a pretty young woman who was presumed to be his daughter. In the course of the next hour Clancy picked up additional details about them. The man looked like an important citizen, even though he was distinctly on the short side, and the girl was a real beauty. She was dark, attractively built, and obviously a stranger to the country. They were staying at the Valley House, Tinaja's only hostelry which made any pretense of respectability. That much Clancy accepted as fact; the rest was conjecture on the part of the men who were doing the reporting.

Then came the big explosion of the day. A man slammed hard into town, keeping his bronc at a full gallop until he pulled up hard before the door of the Miners' Bank. It was the beak-nosed Turk, his dull eyes a little wild with the excitement that had come upon him as he made his fast ride. Men tried to appear casual at the sight, but there was a general movement toward the bank as the loungers scented a new move in the game they could not yet understand. If Turk had galloped into town in such a pucker as this it seemed certain that there must be something important behind his ride. In every mind there was the obvious thought that it had something to do with El Diablo Negro. Diablo had gone into the foothills. Circle D was in that direction. So Diablo must have something to do with Turk's errand.

The crowd was waiting expectantly when Turk came out of the bank again. He stared sullenly at the upturned faces, his slack-jawed scowl making him look more than ever like some kind of grotesque reptile. A few of the more curious loungers hailed him with offers of a drink, knowing the surly one's fondness for making uproarious celebrations out of his infrequent visits to

Tinaja. Turk merely grunted, making no reply to the fire of questions as he climbed into the saddle and forced his way through the crowd. There was a mutter of perplexity as he started away, but then the crowd began to understand. Turk went only a short distance, dismounting again to enter the little office which Marshal Abe Kline maintained at the front end of the town calaboose. The surly one was out of sight for less than five minutes, reappearing to mount and ride slowly out of town in the direction of Circle D.

It left the gossipers with plenty of new fuel, particularly when Abe Kline came hurrying up the street to enter the bank. Everyone understood that Abe took his orders from Chandler Brack, a fact more or less to be expected from the banker's financial position in the valley. Still it was a little amusing to note the marshal's anxious haste as he answered the boss' summons.

Kline's session with Brack lasted nearly an hour, but long before it was over there was a shift of interest. Word went out that Turk had slipped back into town after dodging Brack's possible observation and was tanking up at the Palo Duro. Since his surprising marriage to Mamie Rook there had been precious few opportunities for him

88

to have his fling so it was expected that he would really let himself go.

There was a general descent upon the saloon and soon a dozen men were plying the sullen one with drinks, trying to get the full story out of him before Brack or Boone Sabbath could interfere. It was clear that Turk was trying to keep something a secret, but they soon got enough out of him to believe that the whole thing had been a mistake. He let them know that he had brought a message to Brack from Dimmick, the manager of the Three Toes Mine, and the interest quickly shifted. A mystery man in town was all right as a source of gossip, but important developments in a gold mine were even better. For the time being El Diablo Negro was practically forgotten.

Presently the outside watchers reported that Kline had gone back to his office and had sent Shorty O'Leary, a Brack henchman who held the post of deputy marshal, on some kind of errand across the valley toward the Javelinas. Coupling that with the labored hints Turk had passed made it easy to guess that O'Leary was on his way to the Three Toes.

Noontime had brought its full heat to Tinaja when Turk staggered away from the Palo Duro's bar and was hoisted into his saddle. He was almost genial by that time, quite pleased with the fact that he had slipped one over on Brack, and on Mamie. In a less definite fashion he felt that he had been pretty smart. He hadn't said a word about the reported gold strike in the supposedly dead mine. What never occurred to him was that he had said absolutely nothing about the source of the message. No one had said anything to him about a mysterious black-clad rider so he had given it no thought. To him a Mexican was a Mexican, nothing more, and he didn't even suspect that anyone might be interested in the character of the man who had turned up at Circle D with the message from Dimmick.

It was while Turk was being sent noisily on his homeward journey that a drowsy-looking young fellow on a ragged, unkempt bay pony drifted into town. So many men were in the back alley watching Turk's departure that the newcomer arrived almost unnoticed. He tied his burr-coated bronc at the hitching rack in front of the Palo Duro, listening with no apparent interest to the clatter of voices from the back yard. Dismounting lazily he stretched his long legs and stared about him with the sort of curiosity that a casual stranger might have. He even kept his expression indifferent when he heard a man refer to the cause of the uproar behind the saloon. So Turk had not yet returned to Circle D! In a way that was too bad. Those two women at the ranch house must have had a mighty uncomfortable morning.

For a moment he felt rather conscience-stricken but then he forced the thought from his mind. Neither of them rated any sympathy — and he couldn't afford to divert his thoughts from the problem at hand. Right now he had to keep his mind on the fact that he was sticking his neck out in a highly dangerous manner. There must be a dozen men within sound of his voice who could recognize him, and as many more who would shoot him on sight if Chandler Brack should give the word.

Partly to make himself concentrate on the role he was now playing, he stuck one hand into the pocket of the faded Levi's and brought out some loose change, studying the coins briefly before putting the money away again. After that he turned his back regretfully on the Palo Duro's gently swaying doors and lounged across the dusty street to a small but clean-looking eating house which advertised cheap food. The few men who took time from their gossip to notice him saw only a grub line rider who had skipped a drink to make his scanty capital cover a much-needed meal. Their only concern with the tall man's destination was due to the fact that two other strangers had already gone into the place. The brisk little man and the dark-haired girl had come out of the Valley House some minutes earlier and had gone into the little restaurant.

It was something of a surprise for Wayne to find two such obvious tenderfeet in Tinaja, but he greeted them casually and a bit awkwardly. He pulled off the battered Stetson and managed an embarrassed bow in the direction of the girl as he drawled, "Howdy, folks. Kinda hot, ain't it?"

The little man was perspiring freely in his heavy tweeds, but the remark didn't seem to strike home. The girl nodded, offering a quick smile, but the little man merely nodded in abstract fashion, going right on with what he was saying to his daughter. Wayne decided that the stranger was none too happy with the conditions he had found in Tinaja, but that his mind was too occupied with other concerns for him to be paying much attention to his own physical discomforts. He was small but there was a nervous energy about him which hinted at importance. Iron-gray hair worn rather long but with careful barbering matched the brisk military mustache, while the red face and neck suggested a recent and unaccustomed exposure to the sun. His anxious words seemed to bear out that impression.

"I'm really sorry you came along, Vicky. Things are ever so much cruder than I had anticipated. Are you sure the trip hasn't been too much for you?"

The girl laughed quickly, a pleasant merry sound which made Wayne think of sleigh-bells jingling on a frosty New England evening. "I'm not as soft as you think, Father," she scoffed. "If I hadn't been sure I could take care of myself I wouldn't have insisted on coming along to take care of you."

The little man smiled, letting the girl's humor drive away some of his worry. "I'm not so sure about that," he contradicted. "You would insist if you felt like it, regardless of circumstances."

"Anyway, I'm perfectly all right," she insisted. "I'll rest a little this afternoon while you take care of your business with Mr. Brack, and then we'll see if we can find out what Jan is up to." She gave Wayne a side-long glance which hinted that she was not unaware of his presence even though she kept her open attention centered upon her father.

The reference to Brack had caused the tall man to prick up his ears, but he could still find plenty of interest in the girl. He guessed her to be in her early twenties, probably about the same age as that blonde wench at the Circle D. Otherwise there was little resemblance between the two girls. This one was smaller, darker, and evidently more of a lady. He decided that she was cute rather than beautiful, mainly because of the pertly tilted nose, but the effect was pleasant and he studied her covertly while pretending to scan the fly-specked card which served as a bill of fare.

"I'm sorry you ever got interested in that girl," her father complained, dropping back into his air of concern. "She's as wild as they come, and I'm sure she isn't up to any good coming out to this forsaken hole as she did."

"I think she knows exactly what she's doing," the girl defended. "I like her nerve and I intend to look her up."

Wayne decided that this young lady knew her own mind and was not averse to speaking it. The waitress came in then, a brawny, sharp-featured woman who asked bluntly, "What'll it be, folks?"

94

The two strangers asked about the few dishes on the menu, finally giving grudging acceptance to the woman's suggestion of steak. Wayne took care of his own wants with a single word.

"Stew."

The waitress studied him coldly. "Got any money, pilgrim?" she asked, her tone hinting that she had come into contact with saddle bums before.

He pulled out the loose change and displayed it on a flat palm. "Enough?"

"It'll do. Ye want coffee?"

"How much?"

"Nothin' extra."

"I'll take it."

The woman started back toward the kitchen, but was stopped by the brown-haired girl. "Excuse me," the stranger said, "but could you tell me whether a blonde young woman has come to Tinaja within the past few days? I'm looking for a friend of mine who is supposed to have started in this direction."

The waitress betrayed no sign of interest, her face stolid as she turned to ask, "Was she alone?"

"I suppose so."

"Then I wouldn't know. I don't keep no

track o' loose wimmen what come to this town."

She left abruptly after the crisp statement, her hearers maintaining a flat silence for several seconds. Finally it was the girl who uttered an angry little laugh. "I guess I'd better do my asking somewhere else," she said wryly.

"Maybe you shouldn't ask," her father retorted. "That hint certainly seemed broad enough."

The girl was not to be daunted. She turned to look straight at Wayne, her hazel eyes studying him frankly and with a shade of defiance as she asked, "What about you, mister? Am I asking for another slap if I try the same question on you?"

He gave her a friendly grin. "I'd admire to oblige yuh, ma'am," he drawled, "but I don't know nothin'. I jest blew into town about ten minutes ago. A feller can't get acquainted with too many gals in that amount o' time, yuh know."

"I think you'd better drop the subject," the short man said, a shade of authority entering his voice.

The girl smiled at Wayne, then ignored him completely, and went back to the talk with her father. "I guess I lose. When are we going out to have a look at the mine?"

"Don't be in too big a hurry. I haven't bought it yet."

"But you intend to, don't you?"

His smile was indulgent. "That remains to be seen. I didn't get my reputation by making blind purchases, and I'm certainly not going to start now."

"But there isn't any question about the mine being a good one, is there?"

"Not so far as records can show. It has been producing well for a little over two years now. Still I want to see it before I commit myself." He hesitated before adding, "And you had better let me do any further asking about that girl. Until we find out more about her it might prove embarrassing for you to find her."

The stern waitress returned then, bringing soup for the strangers and a plate of hash for Wayne. There was a brief instant in which Wayne caught the girl's interested glance upon him and then silence descended upon the dining room. It persisted through the short period Wayne needed to consume his meal and was broken only when he got up to pay his bill and go out.

"Sorry I couldn't help," he told the girl. "Mebbe yuh'll be luckier next time."

"Thanks." The word was short enough, but he decided that she would be willing to extend the conversation at some future time. At least that was what her eyes told him.

He slipped out as quietly as he had come in, strolling along up the street in an aimless manner until he reached the stagecoach station which was also the express office. There he paused long enough to make a thoughtful inspection of the reward poster. Then, smothering the ghost of a smile, he went into the building.

"Howdy," he drawled, stretching the Southwestern accent to the breaking point. "Did a gent name of Moss blow into town today?"

The rotund clerk bobbed his head affirmatively. "On the morning stage."

"Know where he might be holed up?"

"Yep. I reckon I do. Leastways his bags went to the Valley House."

Back on the street once more Wayne ambled along slowly, his indolent gait in sharp contrast to the fierce tempo of his thoughts. Ever since he had used that story about the Three Toes Mine as a means of getting rid of Turk he had been thinking about what Mamie had said. At first he had been merely gratified that he should have hit upon such a good story for diversion purposes. Then he began to consider the possibilities for the future. If there was some sort of crooked deal in progress he might find a way to use the fact in his campaign against Brack. He didn't yet know how he was going to handle the information, but he had at least learned the important part about it. Mamie's mention of Moss' name had been the key to the puzzle, and now he felt certain that Brack was trying to sell a worn-out mine to the Easterner.

He turned in at Ben Arms' hardware and general supply store, a little dubious about the extra chances he would be taking if he made such a change in his plans. It would be fine to put a spoke in Brack's wheel — and it would be pleasant to earn the gratitude of a pretty girl like Moss' daughter — but the added risk was a bad one. For one thing it was taking him directly into contact with a Tinaja man who might easily recognize him. Ben Arms had known him pretty well in the old days, and Ben was not the man to keep anybody's secret. Still he went on into the store. A little extra gamble in a desperate game like this was nothing to get excited about.

6

The store was gloomy even in the glare of midday, and Wayne kept the ragged hat brim low as he grunted a reply to Ben Arms' cheery greeting. "I need a mite o' writin' paper," he announced, letting the drawl have full sway. "Nothin' very fancy, jest writin' paper and a envelope. Got 'em?"

"You bet," Ben assured him, reaching back toward a convenient shelf. "Want me to write the letter fer yuh? I do it fer a lot o' the boys."

"I reckon not." The tone of the reply discouraged any further offers. "I reckon I kin spell out what few words I gotta use. Mind if I spread out on yer counter fer a couple o' minutes?"

"Help yourself." Arms took the coppers the customer was offering and went back toward the rear of the store to continue with some unpacking which had been interrupted by Wayne's entrance. He knew a queer feeling which he could not explain, a feeling that he ought to know this tall young fellow. Not that it was surprising. A shopkeeper had to meet a lot of folks in the course of a year's trading, even in a back country settlement like Tinaja, so he couldn't be expected to remember all of them. Still he looked thoughtfully around several times while the stranger was busy with his writing, not giving up on his hunch until the customer grunted a brief "Thanks" and went out.

Back on the street Wayne slouched along as he had done before, making himself as inconspicuous as possible and blaming himself mentally for the added risk he was running. With his whole future, his very existence, depending upon his avoiding recognition he had entered upon an escapade which might prove his undoing. In a way it was even useless. Moss had indicated that he was not in any great rush to close the deal with Brack, and it seemed likely that Brack would likewise hesitate now that he had received the false message.

"Plumb stupid when I ought to be smartest," Wayne told himself. However, he did not hesitate. Having successfully passed through the hazardous business of meeting Ben Arms, he felt a little more confident of his disguise. Better to get this extra chore over; it might pay off well.

No one paid any attention to him as he went on down the street past the main cluster of saloons. The Valley House was almost at the end of the street, keeping itself aloof in its shabby respectability. Wayne knew the place well enough and knew the proprietor, an eccentric sort of character who kept the place running in a profitless manner simply because it made a home for him.

The place was darker than the hardware store had been and Wayne entered cautiously, thinking the front room empty until his eyes accustomed themselves to the gloom and he could see the sleepy-looking man with immense gingery sideburns and a shining bald head who was poring over a battered ledger. Wayne put on his best slouch as he moved toward the desk, keeping the sorry Stetson low over his eyes.

"Got a letter for Mister Moss," he announced lazily. "Feller on a black hawss asked me to bring it."

He dropped the envelope on the desk and was heading back toward the front door before the bald man could gather his wits to ask a question. "Somebody in town, you mean?" the hotel man finally shouted after his retreating visitor.

"Nope." The reply was mumbled over a retreating shoulder. "A feller I met along the Verde foothills. Didn't know the jigger, but he looked like a Mex."

The bald man stammered another query but received no reply. The messenger was already out of the building.

Wayne drew a deep breath of relief as he headed back up the street without having the hotel man come out to hail him. That was that! Catching Al Hulett napping over his bookwork had been just plain lucky. The job had gone off so quickly that there had been no time for the bald man to see his visitor's face. Maybe the big risk wasn't going to be so bad after all.

Clinton Moss and his daughter returned to the Valley House as soon as their meal was completed. They had been intending to look around Tinaja a little, but a very few minutes on the streets had caused them to change their minds. For one thing it was too hot for comfort. For another, Tinaja's siesta hour had turned into a drinking session. The excitement of the day had started it and now the town was getting pretty noisy.

Loose-tongued loungers appeared at saloon doors to stare at the two strangers, their remarks perfectly audible both to the girl and to her father. Most of the remarks were complimentary enough, but their style was definitely on the rough side.

"A fine town for a girl to enter alone," Moss said shortly as they ended their annoying promenade. "I hope you see what it means now."

She did not reply. They entered the hotel and quickly found themselves confronted by something else to occupy their minds. The bald-headed proprietor came across the room to meet them, flaunting a white envelope. "Letter for yo', Mr. Moss," he announced. "A messenger just brought it. Said a man on a black horse sent it from somewhere out in the hills. I didn't have a chance to get any more out of him. He just dropped the letter and ducked out."

He waited expectantly, but Moss simply took the letter and said, "Thank you." Evidently the part about the man on the black horse had been wasted. Perhaps Moss hadn't even heard of El Diablo Negro. Certainly his next comment hinted that he was thinking along quite different lines. "Somebody must have known I was coming. Do you happen to know whether Mr. Chandler Brack is in town today?"

"Sure. He was at the bank most of the

mornin'.""

"Thank you," Moss said again. He gave no indication of the perplexity which had come to him. Brack was the only man who could have anticipated Moss' arrival in Tinaja, but Brack was not out of town. Then who could have written the letter?

The girl seemed about to comment but a glance at her father's face stopped her. She followed him quietly to the bare staircase, taking the lead as he stepped aside for her. Only in the upper hallway did she break the silence to ask, "What do you suppose this means? Is it a woman's writing?"

"We'll soon find out," he said shortly. "But if your friend Jan is in trouble I'm afraid we'll have to leave her that way. I didn't come out here to rescue rattle-headed girls who don't have sense enough to take care of themselves. Come into my room while we have a look at this."

He was ripping the envelope open even as his daughter closed the door. "Clean envelope," he commented. "I wouldn't say this had been carried around the country so much. It isn't even wrinkled." He drew out a single page of cheap paper, exclaiming in surprise at sight of the printed capital letters which made up the message. At the moment he could not know that similar letters

105

had appeared on the back of a poster in the Miners' Bank and were now awaiting discovery on a mirror at the Circle D ranch house. The note was specific and right to the point.

"MR. MOSS,

YOU ARE ABOUT TO BUY A WORN-OUT MINE. THE THREE TOES PETERED OUT SEVERAL MONTHS AGO BUT BRACK HAS BEEN SALTING IT TO KEEP UP PRODUCTION RECORDS. YESTERDAY HE WOULD HAVE SOLD TO THE FIRST SUCKER HE COULD FIND. TODAY HE HAS BEEN TOLD THAT A NEW VEIN OF ORE HAS COME TO LIGHT. WATCH HIS ACTIONS AND SEE HOW HE DELAYS ANY SALE UNTIL HE LEARNS THAT THIS IS A FALSE REPORT. JUST A FRIENDLY WARNING FROM

EL DIABLO NEGRO"

"What's all this?" Moss snapped. "Is somebody playing games around here? Who's El Diablo Negro?"

"Are you asking me?" the girl asked dryly.

He shook his head, ignoring her reply as the anger mounted within him. "It's either a stupid joke or there's something mighty crooked going on in this business. I'm go-

106

ing right out and ask some questions."

He was already storming toward the door when his daughter caught his arm. "Don't," she said, a little sharply. "There may be more to this than meets the eye. Someone seems to have gone out of his way to send you this word, even giving you a sign to check by. Why not play a little cat-and-mouse with this man Brack?"

Moss turned, frowning thoughtfully. "Sometimes you almost make sense, Vicky," he muttered. "Maybe it would work better that way. I'll pretend to be in a hurry to close the deal. If he stalls for a time and then gets anxious to sell I'll know this letter was right."

"That's the idea."

He grinned a little more easily as he caught her smile of satisfaction. "You sound almost smart at times, Vicky. Try to stay that way until I come back, will you? In other words don't wander out on the streets alone."

He went out promptly, not giving her any opportunity to argue the point.

Chandler Brack had spent an uneasy morning. The Diablo matter had been enough to upset him more than he cared to admit, and it had come at a bad time, just when he was expecting a visit from a prospective purchaser for the worn-out Three Toes Mine. With the two subjects battling for top billing in his thoughts he had been thoroughly annoyed when Turk arrived with that message from Dimmick.

The annoyance had been only momentary, however. He forced himself to put the Diablo matter out of his mind, assuring himself that Sabbath and Kline would take care of it efficiently enough. Better to concentrate on the prospective sale. Unlike the rest of Tinaja he had not missed the point about the man who had brought the message to Circle D. Judging by Turk's description it had been El Diablo himself. That meant a trick of some sort and Brack did not propose to play into the enemy's hands by biting at the bait.

Still he didn't want to make any mistakes. If the courier had not been Diablo the story would probably be truthful — and Chandler Brack was not the man to sell a gold mine that was still producing. He had gone to considerable expense in keeping up the illusion of production while angling for such a buyer as Clinton Moss so he wanted to cash in on the false records as quickly as possible. On the other hand he didn't want to sell anything which might be of future value.

Hence Turk's message caused him to spend a mighty restless hour.

Word had come to him that Moss was in Tinaja so he knew that he would have to reach a decision before Shorty O'Leary could return from the Javelinas with verification of the report. It meant he would have to delay matters. But maybe that would not be too difficult. Moss certainly wouldn't try to close the deal without seeing the property. That would afford ample opportunity for getting the truth from Dimmick.

Having reached that conclusion he was in reasonably good spirits when Lum Alsop announced that Moss was waiting to see him. "Send the gentleman in, Lum," Brack boomed pompously. "And see that we are not disturbed."

Moss came in briskly, offering his hand and passing the time of day in a rather restrained manner. Then he went straight to the point. "You're ready to deal on the terms mentioned in our correspondence, I suppose?"

Brack let his eyebrows lift in an expression of surprise that was not entirely simulated. This was just exactly what he had not expected. His reply was smooth, however. "Naturally. But I didn't suppose you were planning to make any settlement until you

109

had seen the mine."

"What would I know about the looks of a mine? All that counts with me is production figures. Naturally I've checked that end of it pretty thoroughly."

"But I would hardly feel right to complete the deal until I felt sure that we understand each other and that you will be perfectly satisfied. It isn't the way I do business. Complaints after the deal is closed are always so much trouble to all concerned. I want to have everything open and above-board."

He almost made it sound perfect. Moss had listened to many a crooked spiel and he knew all of the little dissonances which usually spoiled the tune, but it was hard to spot any flaw in Brack's protestations. Maybe he talked a little too much but there was nothing else suspicious about it. Either the mysterious note writer was all wrong, or this Brack was a pretty smooth character.

Moss studied him coolly. "Then you don't want to close now?" he persisted.

Brack shook his head. "Let's put it this way. We'll ride out this afternoon and see the mine. It's not too far — if you haven't had more traveling today than you care to take. Then we'll talk turkey this evening."

Moss found his suspicions growing even

though the miner-banker made it all sound very plausible. Before he could reply, however, there was a commotion in the street and Brack jumped from his chair to stare out of a side window. Moss also looked out, in time to see a burly gorilla of a man slamming a lathered horse to a sliding halt in front of the bank.

"Damn that turtle-nosed fool!" Brack exclaimed aloud. "What does he think he's doing, coming back here now?" He hurried from the private office, trying to get out and get the door closed before Turk could say something that might be fatal to the sale prospects.

Moss was not passing up any bets, however. He followed Brack into the main part of the bank just as Turk hurled himself through the front door.

"Boss, there's hell to pay!" the excited one burst out. "That dam' greaser musta been lyin' about the mine. He cleaned out the house as soon as I was outa sight. Left Mamie tied up like a bundle o' rags. The other gal, too."

Brack hastened to shut off any further reference to the mine affair. "What did he take?" he demanded.

"Grub and stuff. I didn't wait to find out fer sure. Soon as I cut the wimmen loose I

111

forked a bronc and high-tailed it right back here. Mamie says yuh better not believe that about —"

"Shut up!" There was thunder in the command and Turk subsided abruptly. Brack advanced upon his henchman, reaching out a broad hand to fasten it in the slack of Turk's sweaty shirt. "So you came right back, did you? Then how does it happen you've been gone nearly four hours? Answer me that!"

Turk clawed at the hand which was holding him, struggling not as a big man in the grip of an equally powerful one but futilely as a child might have done. "Honest, boss," he whined, "I didn't figger I needed to hustle. I jest stopped fer a drink or two with the boys before I rode back to the house. I didn't —"

Brack flung him backward. "I'll soon find out if you're lying — and you'd better not be! Now get the hell out of here and find Abe Kline. Tell him what happened. Tell him I want a posse on Diablo's trail just as soon as he can get one together. Do you understand that? Now get out. And don't talk to anybody but Kline. Git!"

Turk gulped, glanced once at Clinton Moss, and hurried away. Even in his slow brain, still extra slow from the drinking,

112

there came a thought. Maybe he had spilled the beans about the mine. He'd better get away before Brack became any more angry than he was. It wasn't healthy to make mistakes like that when you worked for Chan Brack.

The banker forced himself to a studied calmness as the blundering Turk went out. Reaching for the expensive black Stetson which was always worn with the frock coat, he bowed politely toward Moss. "I hope you'll excuse me, Moss," he said with as much smoothness as he could muster. "A particularly troublesome bandit has just raided my residence and I'd like to make sure that proper steps are taken to apprehend him. Where may I find you so that we can get on with our business as soon as this bit of trouble is cleared up?"

"I'm at the Valley House," Moss replied. Then he added, with a dryness which escaped the somewhat abstracted Brack, "You don't need to hurry."

Brack hurried out, his self-control wearing a little thin as he began to realize the implications in this raid upon the Circle D ranch house.

Within a quarter hour most of Tinaja's available manpower was organized into a posse. Mention of Diablo had fanned the old interest into a new liveliness, and there was a general rush to take part in the manhunt which Brack was whipping up so furiously. It was an enthusiastic posse and a remarkably happy one. No one had any particular reason to feel anger or hatred against the black outlaw; it was simply a case of wanting to be on hand when the bold fellow was laid by the heels. Men wanted to know why he had advertised himself so stupidly and why he had made the serious error of raiding the home of the valley's most influential citizen. In many cases there was a secondary consideration, the desire to appear on the same side with Chandler Brack. A man might do himself a lot of good by lining up with Brack and many a posse member had that fact in mind as he volunteered for service.

It was not a well-organized posse. Abe Kline was a poor lawman in the first place, and he had no real authority outside of Tinaja. Brack ignored that point and no one else ventured to mention it. The general result was that a riotous sort of cavalcade fared forth from town, whooping it up until it appeared that Brack and Kline were leading an elaborately comic fox hunt made up of half-drunken riders who didn't know what they were doing, and who didn't care very much. There was plenty of loud enthusiasm, but none of the grim determination which usually characterizes the action of a citizens' posse.

From his position near the door of the Palo Duro, Wayne watched the proceedings with carefully concealed satisfaction. He saw a dozen men trail along after Brack and Kline, headed toward Circle D. Another group, led by Boone Sabbath and a brawny cowpuncher known as Catfish Smith, swung away on a line somewhat to the south of the direction taken by the main body, evidently hopeful of cutting the outlaw's sign in the region where the Circle D punchers had reported seeing him. There were good trackers in both groups, Wayne realized, but he had a feeling that they would not have much luck. They had too many blundering companions to foul up the sign which had already been set to fool them.

If these preparations deserved little but scorn, there was another development which served to remind the watcher of his continuing need for great care. A lone rider had galloped away to the east, driving hard for the Javelinas. Even with the exciting news of Diablo's raid on the ranch house, Chandler Brack had remembered his other problem and had made arrangements for it.

A courier was on his way, either to jog Shorty O'Leary into faster action or to pass the word as to where Brack was now to be found. Wayne realized that the move was characteristic of his enemy. Brack kept thinking all the time; that was what made him so dangerous.

7

The posse had been gone from Tinaja nearly an hour when Vicara Moss decided to go out in search of her father. Once she had seen him from the window of her room, but after that there had been so much excitement that she had completely lost sight of him. There had been such a frenzy of riding out there in the street that she had been quite alarmed, but after a time the riders all disappeared. She was curious about the source of the excitement but, more than that, she was worried about her father. Now that the town was quiet again it seemed like a good idea to go out and find him.

Al Hulett eyed her disapprovingly as she came down the stairs. At least he looked disapproving. Al could appreciate a pretty girl as well as the next man, but he knew Tinaja. This was no time for Vicara Moss to venture out on the street. Men had been drinking pretty steadily since early morning and some of the hardest drinkers were the ones who had remained behind when the posse left.

He frowned his doubts but she ignored them, asking briskly, "Have you seen my father lately, Mr. Hulett?"

"Nope. But he'll be along directly. Yo' better wait here for him."

"Why? What's all the excitement?"

Hulett shrugged. "El Diablo Negro again."

"Who?"

"Just a crazy outlaw who's been stirrin' up the town today. Everybody was all in a pucker this mornin' because the loco pest rode into town and posted a batch o' signs offerin' rewards for his own arrest. Then we just got word that he made a one-man raid on Chan Brack's Circle D ranch house. The boys have gone out to dab a loop on him so he won't get so brash in the future."

"He sounds crazy, all right," she agreed. "Is he a local character?"

"Nope. That's the queer part. He never put on no kind of a show in this territory before, so far as I know, but he shore started off with a loud bang when he opened up for business. Tryin' to make himself a quick reputation hereabouts, mebbe."

She seemed interested, so he killed time by relating all the gossip he had heard about

118

El Diablo Negro. At first he talked simply to keep her from going out on the street but then he discovered that she was interested, even to the point of asking questions. What he couldn't know was that she was trying to find something in his talk which would explain the action of Diablo in sending that letter to her father. Had it been simply a symptom of his general insanity, or was there some pattern of reason behind the day's antics?

"By the way," she murmured, when Hulett seemed about to run out of talk. "There was a note left here for my father a short time ago. He was a little curious about how it came to be delivered. Did he ask you anything about the messenger who left it?"

"Nope. I wasn't here when your father went out."

"Then maybe I should ask you. He'll expect me to be able to tell him, of course. He's that way, always thinking I'll pick up every useless scrap of information which he neglects to get for himself." Her smile made it all seem casual and vaguely amusing. Hulett caught the full force of the smile and nodded quick approval.

"Can't tell yo' much. It was jest a messenger, and I didn't get too good a look at him. Tall man, not very old. Looked kinda like a grub line rider, if yo' know what I mean."

"I'm afraid I don't."

"A saddle bum. Cow country hobo. No regular job, but just ambling around the country, grubbin' on any cow camp that will stand for a handout."

"I see. The sort of man who might take on an errand for a few cents in cash money?"

"That's the idea. Only this gent didn't look quite as down and out as most of 'em. He was dusty and a bit ragged, but I got a good enough look at his face to figure he wasn't too long past a good clean shave."

"And did he tell you where he got the letter?"

"Yep. That's the funny part. He claimed a man gave it to him along the foothills of the Sierra Verdes. They're the mountains west of town, the mountains where El Diablo Negro went when he left here this mornin'. And the feller said it was a man on a black bronc what gave him the note."

If he expected her to bite on that one he was disappointed. She merely said, "Father couldn't imagine who sent the letter. But I don't suppose it was important." Privately she was quite excited. Everything seemed to point to the note actually having come from this peculiar outlaw who had been turning the town inside out. But how had he known about the Clinton Moss angle and why had he interfered?

She turned toward the front door and Hulett recalled his purpose in doing so much talking. In his interest over the affairs of El Diablo Negro he had completely forgotten that he wanted to keep her in the building. "Better stick around the place, Miss Moss," he said soberly. "There's no lawman in town right now and some o' the boys have been lappin' up the licker mighty hard today."

She studied him with a slight frown. "I think I'll be safe enough," she said, a little impatiently. "It's broad daylight and I'm not exactly a child."

"That's just it. This here ain't no town for gals without company."

It reminded her of the other errand she had almost forgotten. Coming back a step or two she asked, "Do you know anything about a girl named Janice Knight? She is supposed to have come here just recently." Then she added a little defiantly, "Alone."

Hulett's broad face was a study. "I don't know her," he said shortly.

Vicara Moss turned away from him once more and went straight out into the glare of the afternoon sun. The hotel man slapped at his hat with some show of irritation, cramming it hard over the bald head as he followed the girl.

Perry Wayne had enjoyed himself quite nicely for the few minutes while Brack and Abe Kline were getting the posse on the trail. It was always fun to outwit an enemy, especially a smart one like Chan Brack. After the posse departed, however, Wayne found himself somewhat less amused but still distinctly interested in the strange actions of a burly cowpuncher named Rory Finnegan. A chance word overheard from a passing citizen had given Wayne his first tip on the man, and the resulting observation had been somewhat enlightening. Now he knew that Finnegan was the ramrod for the current Circle D string of thugs. While Conree operated the ranch and really handled the cattle business, Finnegan bossed the assorted gunmen who were on the payroll pretending to be cowboys. Just now, however, the big, buck-toothed redhead seemed to have another job. He had been sticking very close to Clinton Moss ever since the moment when the bank conference was interrupted. Oddly enough, Moss did not seem to object, even though Rory was more than a little drunk.

It was Finnegan who had promoted a trip to the Palo Duro, and Wayne had tagged idly along, taking a seat in a corner to watch the half dozen men who ranged themselves along the bar, most of them showing the effects of the day's drinking. It was interesting to watch the performance of the bartender, evidently a hand-picked employee of Boone Sabbath or Brack. He was pouring drinks for the other men just as fast as he could take orders, but he protested uneasily when Finnegan began to hit the liquor too hard.

Wayne recognized the full meaning of it. Here was one of the factors which made Brack's hand such a hard one to beat. Every little knot in his organization was snug. Even a bartender had his orders to make sure that a fellow like Rory Finnegan didn't get too drunk to take care of his assignment.

Moss, meanwhile, was not drinking. Wayne suspected that the Easterner was playing some sort of waiting game of his own, probably recognizing the fact that Finnegan was trailing him. It put Moss in a different light, but before Wayne could decide about him there came an open break between Finnegan and the bartender.

"No more, Rory," the apron told him,

almost pleading. "I got my orders, yuh know."

"T'hell wit' yer orders!" Finnegan snorted, his brogue thickening under the influence of the whisky. "Either I git me another drink here or I go off gallivantin' somewhere else. I ain't the bucko to git told off."

"No more from me," the barman insisted doggedly.

Finnegan hurled his empty glass at a shelf full of bottles and fairly flung himself out through the door. "Damn that Boone Sabbath! It's too dom' nosey he is, begorra!"

He disappeared from view, and Wayne heard his complaining tone change sharply. Evidently the big Irishman had found something to his liking on the other side of the swinging doors. "Wurra, wurra, it's me lucky day! Good meetin' to yez, colleen. And where might yez be goin' so swate and sassy?"

Wayne was already on his way to the door when he heard a woman's voice snap a reply. "Go away, you brute. You're drunk!" He knew that it was the voice of the girl he had seen in the eating house. Evidently Clinton Moss also recognized the tones for he was just a step behind Wayne at the doorway.

Vicara Moss had stepped back, evading the groping paws of the drunken gun boss, but Finnegan lurched after her and clamped down hard on one of the slender wrists. "Mebbe I ain't so drunk," he argued. "Jest mighty happy to meet a purty gal like yerself. When did yez arrive and where at are yuh holed up?"

Her answer was a stinging slap to the flushed, unshaven face. The fingers left white welts on the red skin and the big man's foolish grin disappeared. "None o' that, ye domned female blatherskite," he growled, yanking her toward him. "Don't be gittin' high and mighty with Rory Finnegan, me foine chicken. I ain't —"

No one ever found out what he wasn't. The words were blotted out with swift suddenness as a solid fist connected with the side of his head. He rocked sideways, losing his hat as he lost his grip on the girl, and catching his balance only with a stern effort. Then he straightened up, glaring at the ragged-looking young fellow who had dared to lay hands on him.

"Why damn yore eyes!" he growled wrathfully. "I'm jest about gonna kill yuh fer that, pilgrim!"

The drunken grin was gone completely now, the sobering effect of the girl's slap

125

having been seconded by the subsequent blow. He was sober enough to be deadly, and just drunk enough to be thoroughly vicious. Wayne realized the fact and set himself for a rough time. The two men were pretty well matched as to height and weight. A fight between them would be a real matter of skill, endurance and plain ferocity.

Finnegan came in fast, throwing a hard right that would have felled a steer had it connected. Wayne side-stepped without apparent effort or haste, ignoring the blow as he said quietly, "Better go home, brother. Even in Tinaja I hear it ain't considered polite to make passes at a lady."

By that time the scene was attracting an audience. There were still enough men in town to appreciate a fight, most of them drunk enough to whoop it up even before they learned the nature of it. They encircled the contestants as Finnegan turned for another rush, their jeers seeming to incite him to greater wrath. He had to do something about this lanky saddle bum who had slugged him and then made him look foolish before witnesses.

He cursed bitterly and started another lunge, aiming his blows a little more carefully this time. Again the black-haired man evaded the flurry of blows, but instead of using further words of caution he sent in a hard, fast jab that caught Finnegan flush on the point of his blunt chin. Most of the on-lookers were not even sure they had seen the blow struck, but all of them knew they had heard the thud of its impact on Finnegan's jaw. Rory's head snapped back and he tottered for an appreciable instant. Then he went down hard on the seat of his pants.

Somebody laughed and a man jeered drunkenly, "Yuh better git back to Circle D, Rory. This shore ain't yore cup o' tea."

Finnegan rolled swiftly, shaking his head as he came up for another onslaught. To the accompaniment of much ribald merriment he launched his body in another vicious charge, trying to beat down his antagonist under sheer weight of anger. This time Wayne came to meet him, going into a quick crouch which permitted him to duck a powerful but awkward swing. Almost in the same motion he threw in two more of those lightning punches. A hard left to the midriff doubled Finnegan up and the follow-up right fairly lifted the cowboy off his feet. Finnegan went over backwards, crashing hard to the well-packed dirt sidewalk, and stayed there.

Out of the resulting uproar a voice rose sharply. "Better git outa sight, young feller.

Finnegan's goin' to wake up mighty sore —
and next time he ain't goin' to fight with
fists. He'll come up shootin'!"

Wayne nodded, still keeping his eyes on
the prone man in front of him. "Thanks,
but I'm packin' a gun myself." Then he realized almost absently that the warning
voice had been familiar. Looking up quickly
he saw that it was Al Hulett who had
spoken. The hotel man was excited enough,
but there was something else behind his
glance — something that Wayne did not like
to think about. Even granting that Hulett
was displaying signs of friendship it was not
comfortable to be flirting with recognition.

A couple of men moved in then, grabbing
Finnegan by the shoulders and dragging
him into the cooler regions of the Palo
Duro. They paid no open heed to Wayne,
but he was not deceived. They were Brack
men and would report and describe the
stranger who had dared to take issue with a
Brack lieutenant.

It was Vicara Moss who broke in on the
swift flow of ominous thought. "I want to
thank you for taking my part so splendidly,"
she told him, flashing the smile which he
had noted with such pleasure. "That brute
was drunk enough to be entirely unreason-
able."

Wayne grinned. "Yeah," he agreed. "I noticed that." He was trying to find a way out of the dangerously conspicuous position in which he had placed himself, but at the same time he hesitated to pass up this opportunity to get acquainted with the girl. His reason, he tried to tell himself, was that it would be rather suspicious for him to break away too hastily.

Clinton Moss also tried to express his thanks, but the girl gave him no opportunity. She took a couple of steps toward Wayne, making no attempt to conceal her feeling. "Don't try to joke about it. You did something very wonderful, and my father and I would like very much to have you come and dine with us this evening."

Wayne shook his head, a little embarrassed at what he saw in her eyes and also at the way his plans were being upset. It was all right to make impressions on pretty girls, but not at a time like this. Then he realized that Al Hulett was whispering something in Clinton Moss' ear.

The little man frowned in surprise but straightened his expression as he cut in hastily, "Mr. Hulett tells me that he will be able to serve us a meal this evening, so we can dine at the hotel." His voice changed subtly as he added, "I'm sure we can find something interesting to discuss."

Wayne almost missed the girl's eager nod. All he could think about was that Hulett had identified him. He would have to play up to Moss and the girl, hoping to find some way out of the dangerous dilemma.

"You will come, won't you?" Vicky Moss begged, giving him the full benefit of her smile once more.

He met it. "I'm afraid I ain't likely to make much of a hand at talk, but I'd shore admire to sit down to a real good meal again. 'Specially with such a purty gal. Thanks."

He could almost feel the puzzled silence as he turned away and strode toward the hitching rack where the bay pony still awaited him. Several pairs of eyes were watching him curiously while Moss and Hulett were something more than curious. He wished he could know whether Hulett had identified him completely or only as the bearer of the letter from Diablo. One way or another it was not to his liking. Things like that always leaked out, and a leak at this stage of the game would certainly be fatal.

The sidewalk was clearing rapidly when he swung into the saddle and pulled the bay away from the rail. The Palo Duro's loungers had faded back into the dimness of the saloon's interior, only a few remaining to stare. Clinton Moss called, "We'll look for you about six." Then he took his daughter's arm and turned away.

Wayne knew something like a sense of relief but then he caught the full stare of the one-legged man who was studying him from the corner of the building. Pegleg Clancy had shown signs of peculiar interest earlier in the day, and now he seemed even more concerned. That was bad. Clancy had long been a Circle D rider and now he worked for Brack in the Palo Duro.

Even as the thought crossed his mind he saw the light of understanding come into the little man's intense eyes. Pegleg opened his lips as though to call out, then closed them again firmly and continued to stare. Wayne moved away, trouble crowding hard into his thoughts. Tinaja was getting too hot for him.

Prudence dictated a prompt retreat into the hills, but he knew that there were plenty of objections to the course. He didn't want to run afoul of Brack's posse and he understood all too well that his campaign could not be one of retreat. He had to attack — and that meant being on the scene of greatest activity, at least until he had struck home the blows that would turn matters into the proper directions.

Playing the hunch for all it was worth, he turned the bay into the nearest lane, riding around through the series of untidy back yards which flanked the buildings of the main street. Pegleg Clancy had recognized him, but Pegleg had given no alarm. It left him with a hope but no choice. He had to find out where Clancy stood. It would be sheerest folly to leave town until that point was decided.

So far as he could tell no one had seen his sudden move, but he played it as safe as possible, tying the bay at the corner of Ben Arms' rickety old stable and continuing afoot to the adjoining stable where he believed Clancy must be living. Other Palo Duro swampers had been quartered there in the past, so it seemed likely that Clancy would now occupy the place.

The late afternoon quiet worked in his favor, alcohol and heat combining to keep most of Tinaja indoors. No one stirred along the backs of any of the buildings, and he ducked into the Palo Duro stable with the feeling that he had been quite unobserved. Instantly a low voice greeted him from the semi-gloom of the interior.

"Howdy, Perry. I figured yuh'd be along

purty quick."

Wayne didn't bother to deny the identification. "That's why I came," he said shortly. "Because I knew you knew."

Pegleg chuckled, advancing to stick out a gnarled paw. Wayne accepted it, grateful that the little man was showing signs of friendliness. "You're a plumb smart hombre, Clancy," he said. "How'd you happen to tumble?"

"Yuh don't need to spread that drawl on so thick. It was right convincin' but I been kinda curious ever since I noticed the cut o' yer withers this mornin'. I didn't spot yuh then, but I had a sneakin' notion that I oughta know them shoulders. Then I got to thinkin' about the whole dad-blamed performance and I couldn't figger any sensible reason why an outlaw should want to stir up trouble fer hisself. Purty soon I come up with the idea that the whole thing's a cute way of makin' a pass at somebody, most likely Chan Brack. Which made me think of yuh and how yuh might wanta do jest that very thing. Then I knew why that back looked familiar."

"Sounds easy the way you say it," Wayne told him. "I hope nobody else was as smart."

"Yuh had me fooled this afternoon," Clancy went on, taking the compliment in

133

stride. "I didn't look fer yuh to turn up so soon again and in a different outfit. It wasn't 'til yuh hung that fancy right on Rory's whiskers that I woke up."

"You're even smarter than I said," Wayne told him, his casual tone betraying none of the tension he was feeling. "What are you planning to do about it?"

That was the big question and both men seemed to realize it, even though it had been posed in such quiet fashion. Pegleg Clancy was in a position to cause a great deal of trouble for Perry Wayne — if Wayne should permit the little man to stand in his way. Men had died to relieve situations much less critical.

8

Pegleg grinned a bit uneasily, recognizing the peril in his situation. "I was plannin' to throw in with yuh," he said with some earnestness. "I ain't forgot the way Chan Brack let me git busted up and then shoved me into this job. I was doin' his work with no helper but that stupid dam' Turkle. Anybody with half a brain woulda kept me from gittin' smashed up this way, but Brack wouldn't give me no helper but Turk. Which makes it purty much his fault that I got stove up, and all he does fer me is to turn me into a dam' swamper! Nacherly I'm rootin' hard fer anybody what's aimin' to stir up some hot embers around his stinkin' hide."

It was quite a speech for Clancy, the bitterness in it leaving Wayne with scant doubt as to its honesty. He made his decision promptly, realizing that this castoff from the Brack forces might turn out to be a mighty useful ally. Clancy knew a few things even though he probably wouldn't be of much help in a real fight. Still a helper would be most welcome; the job was turning out to be a little awkward for one man.

"Right, Clancy," he said, still maintaining the casual tone. "I'm putting my cards on the table for you and you alone. Do we understand each other on that?"

"I'm mum. But let's climb up to the loft. I got a peephole up there where I kin watch the back o' the hotel. We kin keep an eye on things and have yuh out o' sight if anybody comes snoopin' around."

They climbed to the roost Clancy had prepared, the little man making hard work of it but refusing any help from Wayne. When they were located satisfactorily he said, "Yuhr time to talk, Perry. Tell me what yuh want to; I ain't askin' nothin'."

"I'm giving you the whole thing as I know it," Wayne said. "Part of it I figured out for myself, and part I got from a waddy named Peters. Used to ride for Brack."

"I remember him. Kinda left of a sudden."

"That's right. Brack decided he knew too much so he paid him to leave the basin. I helped Peters when he was in a jam and he told me a few things that I only suspected and some other things I didn't even suspect.

Anyway, Brack framed me for the murder of Josh Lloyd."

"Yuh mean Brack done the killin'?"

"Sure."

"Can yuh prove it?"

"No. That's why I'm having to handle the whole business in this crazy fool style. I know, but I can't prove, that Brack planned to kill Lloyd so he could get complete control of the Three Toes Mine. The gold was running good and Brack wanted it all. So he planned a killing that would appear to be the work of some wandering prospector. I happened to ride into the Javelinas at the time of the murder, and Brack was smart enough to see his chance. He changed his plans to make me the apparent killer."

"Why?"

"Think back a little. At that time Brack was struggling pretty hard to make something of the Circle D while still holding on to that land office. Neither one of them was doing very well and his capital was spread out too thin. One bit of bad luck would have ruined him. It was just then that Josh Lloyd happened along and wheedled a grubstake out of Brack. Two days later he struck it rich.

"It was at that point that Lloyd was too smart for his own good. He didn't want to start a gold rush until he had sewed up everything that looked good, so he kept the news a secret from everyone but his partner. Brack sent him back to develop the mine, making his own plans when he realized that this was his chance to secure for himself enough quick cash for all of the big schemes he had in mind."

Pegleg grunted his understanding. "Always late with the payroll in them days," he muttered. "Seems like it musta been jest like yuh say."

"The plan was simple. Brack rode out of Tinaja one morning, letting several people know that he was going out to see whether Lloyd had hit anything that looked like pay dirt. In a saddle bag he had an old gun that he knew could never be traced to him. He killed Lloyd without a qualm, leaving the gun beside the body. Then he started back to Tinaja to report finding Lloyd as the victim of a mystery killer. That was when I blundered into the picture.

"I was on my way to see Josh Lloyd all right, but I never got that far. I was riding through the gulch about a mile or so short of the creek when somebody took a couple of pot-shots at me. They were close enough to be awkward, but I didn't even suspect that they were carefully planned to be that close and no closer. I spotted smoke in the bushes above the gorge and I saw somebody move up there. Naturally I flung a shot at him for good luck and then tried to run him down. It wasn't any use. He got away clean and after a while I went on toward the Three Toes. It must have been the time I took trying to find the bushwhacker that gave Brack his chance. Anyway he ducked me and circled back to pick up an empty shell where I had ejected it. Then he rode hell for leather back to the mine and changed his plant, picking up the old gun and leaving my empty shell case."

Clancy moved excitedly in the warmth of the loft. "I kin fill it out from there, I reckon. Brack hustled back here to report findin' the body, and when some fellers went out to look the ground over they found that shell. And they hooked it up with Perry Wayne because there wasn't another gun o' that size anywhere in these parts. Brown-Merrill breech loader, wasn't it?"

"You've got a good memory," Wayne told him, his voice grim again. "I kept that gun because it was made in my old home town. Newburyport, Massachusetts. I always thought it might bring me luck — but it almost hung me!"

"Then yuh didn't figger out how it was

'til after yuh broke jail?"

"No. And that's another point. I think it was Brack who fixed it for me to escape. He let the trial go as far as he dared, far enough so that the case was settled against me, but he didn't want me around long enough for me to get any ideas. By getting me to slant out of here, he clinched the case and paved the way for a foreclosure of the property I'd mortgaged to him."

"Right neat little scheme all around," Clancy growled. "Sounds like Brack from start to finish. Not only did he git Lloyd's share o' the gold but he picked up that ranch o' yor'n."

"Which was just enough to get him started toward owning the whole valley."

Clancy was silent for several minutes, staring out of a peephole in the warped front of the stable. "So he owes me somethin' fer the wreck he made of me, and he owes yuh a ranch and a couple o' outlaw years. Mebbe we kin figger out a way to collect. Meanwhile there's somethin' doin' on the street. Yuh better stick close here while I go have a look-see."

He slipped away silently, leaving Wayne to wonder whether he had done right in staking so much on Clancy's good intent. He did not have long to fret, however. Pegleg came back without delay, his unbalanced step sounding in the gathering gloom even before Wayne could see him.

"Might as well come on down," he called softly. "Looks like the town's plumb quiet. That was Dimmick and O'Leary what just rode in. Dimmick's fit to be tied. He don't know what the fuss is all about."

Wayne chuckled under his breath as he slid down to the ground floor of the stable. "He wouldn't. The whole thing was a wild shot of mine that happened to hit straight home." He went on to relate the events of the morning at Circle D, adding for Clancy's interested ear the story of the letter he had delivered to Clinton Moss.

"Yuh shore have been a busy little bee," Clancy told him. "But what sense does it make? Yuh ain't just plannin' to rile Brack, are yuh? That wouldn't do no real good and yuh won't git nothin' but a bullet fer yuhr pains."

"Maybe I'm not doing much better than that," Wayne admitted. "I can't prove anything on him and I can't even step up and make charges. Not while I'm legally just an escaped convict. So I'm sparring, probing for the weak spot in his armor. When I find it I'm hoping I'll see some way to take advantage, and if I can get him mad enough maybe he'll make a mistake that will give me my cue."

"Sounds like a plenty risky proposition to me."

"It is. But I can't see any other chance."

"Well, count me in."

There were no heroics about it. Clancy had simply expressed his own decision after hearing all the facts. Wayne accepted the offer in the same spirit. "I can use you," he told the little cripple. "For one thing I need a pair of eyes in Tinaja, and I need a place to hang out when I'm in town."

"Too easy," Clancy retorted. "I'll start right in by passin' out a bit o' news. I know where Brack got the gold he's been usin' to salt the Three Toes. It's stuff the prospectors have been bringin' in to the bank and depositin' with him. Mebbe yuh kin use it on this feller Moss when yuh go visitin' with him."

"I'm not planning to go. I wouldn't argue with him out there on the street, but I can't take that kind of a chance."

Clancy grinned. "Not even with a purty gal in on the deal?"

"Not even with a purty gal," Wayne assured him, imitating his tone. "Which reminds me. Who is the blonde wench at Circle D?"

"Didn't know there was one there. Heck, I musta been missin' somethin'."

Wayne raised a warning hand against Clancy's lips as a soft footfall sounded from the outer darkness. The two men listened almost without breathing, quickly realizing that some intruder was coming toward the stable, someone whose step hinted that he did not wish to be detected. Clancy shoved Wayne toward a rear corner, whispering quietly, "I'll take care of him. Stay outa sight unless I git more'n I kin handle."

There was just time for Wayne to ease across the dirt floor of the stable and to find a hiding place behind a row of stalls. Then a voice called cautiously, "Yo' in there, Clancy?"

"Where else would I be? What the hell do yuh want?"

"Not so loud. Who's with yo'?"

"Ain't I always alone, yuh pore dumb galoot!"

By that time Wayne knew that the man at the door was Al Hulett. Evidently the hotel man still had something on his mind. And that might turn out to be awkward.

There was a rustle of movement as Hulett came into the stable, then his voice sounded again, clearer this time and a little changed in tone. "I guess yo' know who I'm lookin' for, Pegleg. Might as well forget the dumb act; no use in us foolin' each other when we're workin' on the same side."

Clancy protested again, but Hulett cut him short. "I saw enough this afternoon, Pegleg. That was Perry Wayne who slugged Rory out there, and he holed up in this stable not three minutes later. His bronc is still out there back of Ben's place. Yo' might as well let me talk to him. What I've got to say won't hurt him none, and it might help."

Wayne stepped forward then. "Seems like my disguise didn't amount to much, Al. But then I was afraid all the time that you'd get smart."

Hulett came to meet him, groping for the younger man's hand in the darkness. "Yo' fooled me the first time, Perry, but I couldn't stay dumb forever. How are you, and what kind of crazy game are you trying to pull, coming into town and riskin' yore neck like this?"

Clancy sighed elaborately. "Looks like yuh got some more chin music to make, Perry. I'll git outside and mount guard while yuh tell old baldy the story o' yuhr wicked life."

Wayne smiled in the darkness. It made him feel better to hear the note of cheer in Clancy's voice. The little man had sounded pretty bitter all through their earlier conversation, but for some reason he now seemed more optimistic. Perhaps the prospect of a new ally had done something for him.

It took quite a time to exchange stories with Hulett, but the result was much as it had been with Clancy. Hulett was anxious to see Brack beaten and he was perfectly willing to help an old friend, but he didn't see just how it could be accomplished.

"What I don't savvy," he complained, "is why yo' raised up all this fuss with the Diablo business. It don't make yo' any safer to have every gunman in the valley lookin' for yo'."

"Maybe not, but it seemed like a good way to start my war of nerves. The poster I shoved under the bank door had a message on the back, warning Brack that Diablo was out to get the real killer of Josh Lloyd. I left a similar message when I raided Circle D. I also sent him a shell like the one he used to frame me for Lloyd's murder, and I left another shell like it at the ranch house. I figure all of that coming in such a hurry ought to make him jump around a bit — and it's just possible that he'll make some interesting jumps."

"Where are yo' holed up?"

Wayne told him. "Out there I know the country and I figure I'm pretty safe. The big risk is having somebody spot me here in town. You did it and so did Pegleg Clancy."

"But nobody else, I feel sure," Hulett told him. "Not many folks knew yo' well in the old days. Yo' didn't spend much time in town and all they'd remember was a skinny kid with a Boston accent and a straggly yellow mustache that was supposed to make him look old enough to get a drink of licker if he should happen to want it. A couple o' years has put some pounds on yo' and that black hair fixes the job up complete. Just don't forget yoreself and start spoutin' any poetry."

"What a thing to hold against a man!" Wayne exclaimed. "I'll try to control myself."

"One thing I'd like to know," Hulett said, turning serious again. "I'm not doubting you, understand, but I'd like to clear up the whole business. There was some right nice samples o' gold turned up in yore place after they arrested yo'. Would yo' be wantin' to explain that?"

Wayne laughed shortly. "I don't blame you for asking. It was another sample of the way Chan Brack's luck was running. He got one break when I blundered into a spot where he could pin his own murder game on me. He got another when they found that gold.

146

It made it seem plenty clear that I'd killed Lloyd while robbing the Three Toes."

"I remember that part."

"The gold was mine. I located a small pocket right on my own place. That was why I rode across the valley to see Lloyd. I didn't know anything about gold, and I wanted him to see a sample. After I was arrested I kept quiet about it because I didn't want to start gold hunters stampeding onto my land."

"You mean you kept your secret even though it put yo' in such a nasty spot?"

"Sure. At first I thought the mistake would get straightened out and I wouldn't need to expose my pet secret. By the time I woke up to how bad a spot I was in there wasn't any point in telling the facts. Nobody would have believed me by then. It simply would have resulted in some smart jasper doing some snooping around. So I kept quiet, hoping for the best."

"And yore gold — the bit yo' had on hand, that is — was claimed by Brack as part of the Three Toes property."

"Which is another point on which I owe him something."

"Yo' think he suspected the truth?"

"I feel sure he did. Somebody has been doing some real old searching around my place, almost tearing the house apart in doing it."

"Any trace of 'em findin' anything?"

"No."

Hulett switched topics abruptly. "What about this Moss feller? Are yo' plannin' to hold that confab with him this evenin'?"

"No. My game is to keep as shady as possible, and I can't do myself any good by hobnobbing with the most conspicuous pair of people in town. That was a bad mistake I made awhile ago and I don't propose to repeat it."

"I had an idea the girl was right anxious to see yo' again," Hulett suggested slyly. "And she ain't what yo' call real homely neither."

"I noticed that. But I'm in no position to be getting ideas about women."

"Too bad," Hulett complained. "They're the first good payin' customers I've had in months. I even went out and dug up a cook so they'd stay happy. If I coulda counted on yo' to keep the girl interested I mighta made some dinero out of 'em."

He changed his doleful tone as Wayne laughed, asking suddenly, "Did yo' see another girl out there at Brack's when yo' held yore one-man invasion? This Moss girl was askin' about her and I didn't know what to say."

"You know more than I do," Wayne told him. "There was a girl there, a rather pretty blonde with tough ideas but no judgment. I had to tie her up. Brack's newest, I suppose?"

"That's how I figured it. She just showed up in Tinaja a day or so ago. Went right out to Circle D. That's why I didn't want to talk when the Moss girl asked me. A man can't right out and tell a lady that her old playmate has gone to the dogs."

A warning hiss from Clancy silenced them and they could hear the clatter of horsemen in the street. "Posse comin' in," Pegleg called softly. "Sounds like they're plumb unhappy."

Hulett moved toward the open door. "I gotta get back to the hotel," he said quickly. "I'll be keeping my eyes open. If yo' need help let me know — but don't work me into anything that'll cause us both nothin' but trouble."

Wayne did not even reply. He was wondering whether his talk with Hulett had not been a complete mistake. The hotel man was not a very sturdy ally. Still there hadn't been any real way to avoid taking the bald one into partnership. Hulett had recognized

149

him. From that point the hand had been forced.

Clancy broke in again, whispering hastily as Hulett disappeared in the darkness. "Sit tight, Perry. I'll meander out and give an ear to all the tales of woe. Be right back."

He was gone for something over a half hour, an interval used by Wayne in an effort to clear his own mind and to rearrange his disrupted plans. The program was not going just as he had planned it, and most of the changes were more than a little disturbing to him. The game was becoming more complicated and no particular result was yet in sight.

Clancy was cheerful when he slid back into the stable. "Sounds like yuh shore enough left a cute trail, Perry," he greeted. "Some o' them hombres are ready to believe old Diablo's a shore enough ghost. They're plumb puzzled."

He pieced together the items of information he had picked up. The main posse had stopped at the Circle D ranch house long enough to hear Mamie's sputtering profanity, taking the trail promptly after that. So far as Pegleg had been able to determine no one had seen the blonde girl around the place. Only Brack had entered the ranch house, and he had made it clear that he

150

wanted no one else in there. He had seemed angry enough after taking a look at the place but he simply told his men that Diablo had stolen food, a gun and some ammunition.

The first part of the tracking job had been a cinch. The lead trailers could see where the pack horse had been left, awaiting the load of plunder, and they could trace the raider's path both approaching and leaving the scene of the attack. The double trail led them fairly into the real foothills and then it disappeared completely.

Brack spread his forces at that point, insisting that the trail would be found again at some point where the black rider had been forced to leave rocky ground, but no one had found such a place. The men had spent an hour or so, riding around in circles until even the good trackers were baffled by the multiple trails of their less expert companions. Then they gave up in disgust.

Meanwhile the other contingent had picked up the trail in the more southerly hills where the Circle D boys had reported seeing El Diablo Negro. As with Kline's detachment there was a brief period of easy trailing and then complete confusion. El Diablo seemed to have ridden across the edge of the old Wayne clearing, entering the shallow brook there, but only to ride out again and circle back toward Tinaja. That didn't make sense to any of them. The man certainly didn't think he could throw a tracker off the scent by such a childish trick as that! And what about the raid on Circle D? How had he managed to get over there?

The leaders conferred hastily, reaching the conclusion that the return trail had been a ruse. Diablo had started back toward town but had then cut sharply to the north and made his raid on the Brack place. The move toward the Wayne place had been one blind and the apparent return to Tinaja had been a second one. So they played it smart and headed directly for the Circle D, soon meeting the equally puzzled members of the main posse. By that time Diablo's trail was as completely fouled as though Wayne had given directions for the purpose.

"There's jest about an even split of opinion," Clancy reported with a happy chuckle. "Half of 'em figger yo're a ghost what leaves footprints only when yuh want to. The other half kinda got a suspicion that there's two fellers mixed up in the deal."

"I don't know that I like the latter guess," Wayne told him. "The whole Diablo business was to keep any attention from my true identity. Maybe I over-reached myself a little."

"Don't fret about little points," Clancy retorted. "Yuh got too many big things on the fire. One of 'em is the meetin' Brack has called fer this evenin' in his office. All his main gunnies, I hear. Better start thinkin' how yuh're gonna get an ear on that one."

9

The council of war held in Brack's office that evening was a highly efficient session. Two years had been a sufficient time for Brack to build up an organization of both strength and stability, and tonight it swung into action like a military machine. Counting Brack there were six of them around the desk in the rear room of the bank, the grim expressions indicating that every man was more than a little irritated at the way a loco bandit had played tricks on them. Rory Finnegan's battered countenance showed something more than mere irritation.

"It boils down to this," Brack grated, studying the end of a badly frayed cigar to interrupt the opening rattle of irate talk. "We've got to find out what this Diablo polecat wants. Either somebody is using him for a private purpose or he's got some new game of his own, something the old Diablo never worked. I want to know which it is."

"I still think Diablo's dead," Abe Kline growled, shaking his head until the huge ears almost flapped. "I don't have no truck with ghost talk, but it's either that or somebody puttin' on an act of bein' the old Mex rascal."

"We don't need to worry about that point," Brack told him, a little hastily. "Whether we're dealing with the real Diablo or not won't make any difference. It's the whole game we've got to stop."

Conree's bullet head wagged in a gesture like that of the lanky marshal. "I don't like outlaws what don't make sense," he complained. "A gun-fightin' tough hombre I kin understand, but this Diablo critter bothers me. Why did he bust into town and post them notices about hisself? How did he git in and out without bein' seen? How did he disappear from two different parts o' the hills at the same time without leavin' no trace? I'd like to know some o' them answers before I puzzle my head over anything fancy."

"Don't be a damned fool!" Brack snapped. "Can't you see that the whole thing has been planned to make it look mysterious? Now take it from there. We know he's smart because nobody but a smart hombre could have fouled up his own trail the way he did.

Then we can figure he had a plenty good reason for the rest of the performance. It was supposed to look crazy, but we can bet our pile that it wasn't."

Conree grunted, but made no reply. Brack went on more smoothly, "Now here's another thing we know. He used a smart dodge to get rid of Turk this morning. That means he knows all about the Three Toes. He knows it's a dead claim and he knows I'm trying to unload it. So he's got a connection on the inside. Does that mean anything to you?"

No one was missing the pointed hint. The five men in front of him glanced uneasily at each other but kept their eyes from meeting the stern glare of their leader. It was Dimmick who found his voice first. "If yuh mean me, Chan, it ain't so. I ain't talked to nobody, not even to them horse thieves yuh keep sendin' over to pretend they're workin' the mine."

"Go aisy wit' them names!" Finnegan snapped. "Me byes know their jobs and it ain't fer the likes of yez to be black-guardin' 'em."

"Rats!" Conree cut in disgustedly. "They'd sell their own grandmothers if it meant dinero fer 'em."

Brack made no attempt to stop the

wrangle. He seemed content to watch the play of hate between his lieutenants, and he knew that Boone Sabbath was watching just as closely. None of them was at all slow in recognizing the nature of the organization which had been flung together. Greed had brought them into alliance, and greed could easily cause treason. Every man knew it and was suspicious of every other man.

Finally Brack took over the talk once more, his voice harsh but under good control. "I'm accusing nobody, boys," he said flatly, "but I'm wide open to evidence. You know that, I think. You're with me while I'm making the job pay — and not a damned bit longer. In case somebody thinks he sees a bigger profit in playing up to that black rider let me warn you now that the outlaw's game is due for a quick snubbing. When he winds up on the wrong end of a rope or a bullet just make sure that he don't have company."

"I'm with yuh all the way," Conree assured him hastily. "Jest give us yuhr orders."

"I'm doing just that, and we've got all the law on our side. Diablo made it plumb easy for us, advertising himself the way he did. From now on it's shoot to kill — and on sight."

"That's goin' purty far, Chan," Marshal

157

Abe Kline protested. "I got to make it all look legal, yuh know, and we ain't got nothin' very big on this Diablo jigger." He paused significantly before adding, "Unless yuh're holdin' out on the rest of us."

Brack flashed him a stern but uneasy glance. "What do you mean by that, Abe?"

"Jest what I said. I'm supposed to be the law around here and I ain't hankerin' to git myself fouled up in places I don't know about. Right now I'm figgerin' there's more to this Diablo business than I've heard. Fer one thing, Jabe Conree musta been mighty close to the ranch house this morning when that raid come off. I'm wonderin' why he didn't know it was happenin'."

Conree started to sputter, but Kline went right on without paying any attention to the interruption. "Another thing, there was that poster in the bank. Yuh didn't let anybody look at it fer quite a spell. I'm wonderin' if there wasn't somethin' about it that had to be fixed before yuh let folks see it. Same thing at the ranch house. Yuh was mighty sure that nobody else got in to have a look at the place. If there's anything behind this game that yuh're not tellin' us —"

"Don't be a bigger fool than nature made you, Abe," Brack cut in, his blocky countenance dark and stormy as he stood up, resting white knuckles on the top of the polished desk. "You let me do the thinking for this crew. Meanwhile take my word for it that what I know means nothing to any of you and it won't be dangerous to you in any way. Maybe I even know what Diablo's game happens to be. One way or another I trust none of you that far. Is that clear?"

No one replied.

"I'm assuming it is. I'm also assuming that you will play it my way if you expect to stay healthy."

"We're with yuh, Chan," Kline said hastily. "I jest wanted to know. Now that yuh put it that way —"

"So keep it in mind. I want Diablo's carcass and I want it quick. You can give out that he's the real Diablo and that he went plumb loco after his last brush with the rangers. That ought to take care of the kill-on-sight order. Now, Rory, what about your boys? How many of them are in town?"

"Most of 'em."

"Good. Keep 'em on the streets. So far this Diablo has made us look silly. Folks are laughing at me behind my back, and I won't stand for that. Get your boys on patrol and let these coyotes know I'm still boss around here. Conree, you get out to the spread and take charge there. Keep your men ready for a hurry call. Dimmick, your job is to stick here in town in case I need you. Now get moving!"

Everybody headed for the door with some haste except Boone Sabbath. He remained behind until the others were out of earshot. Then he asked, "Wayne?"

Brack nodded slowly.

"He's back of it but I don't think he's handling the thing. It would be too risky for him to show himself around here. All we can do is hope to smoke him out fast, but we've got to get this partner of his before anything else busts loose."

"Got anything in particular for me?"

"Yeah. Keep an eye on the rest of the boys. Report back to me in an hour. I've got a couple other matters to attend to, things I'd have done today if this damned business hadn't cropped up. You look after affairs in town while I put in a couple of hours here, and we'll pull this job out of the fire pronto."

As Sabbath went out, a shadow detached itself from the wall outside the office window, a tall shadow which moved silently into the blackness behind the building. Wayne had overheard just about what he had expected to hear. The hunt was on and it was to be a merciless one. He could not even take much satisfaction out of spotting the weakness in the ranks. Conree was fearful and Abe Kline was a little on the shaky side, but neither would dare to let fear influence his actions. Rory Finnegan's gunhawks would be on the job to take care of that.

There was an interval of comparative quiet after the men moved away from the building. Wayne still remained in shadow, however, watching the light in Brack's window and turning over tentative plans in his mind. It was becoming grimly clear that if he hoped to break this gang he had to strike faster and harder than now seemed possible. Somehow he had to find that opportunity.

Suddenly he realized that the opportunity was actually at hand. With a little luck and a bit of nerve he might pull off a coup that would make the morning's raid look pale. Acting almost with the thought, he worked his way across the rear of the bank building, scouting both sides and the front before moving out into the street. He hadn't heard any orders given for a hidden guard but he played it safe, keeping shady until he was sure. That was one advantage on his side; Brack and his men trusted each other so little that the leader had to do some of his work completely alone.

Wayne tapped boldly on the window beneath which he had earlier set up his listening post. His summons brought the sound of a quick movement and then Brack's voice came irritably, nervously, as though he had been surprised at some task which would not stand inspection.

"Who's there?"

"Me, boss. Come to the front door. This won't keep." The hoarse whisper was rather well done, Wayne told himself. Plenty of practice in concealing a New England twang and building up two new accents had helped to make imitations rather easy.

"Rory?" Brack asked, his voice dropping to a matching whisper.

Wayne repressed a chuckle of triumph. "Sure. Keep shady and don't make a light out front."

He could hear Brack doing something at the desk and then footsteps marked the man's progress into the outer room of the bank. Wayne braced himself and took the gamble. If anyone should pass along the street within the next couple of minutes it would be just too bad.

His luck held and in a matter of seconds there was the sound of a bolt being shoved back. Wayne poised himself for the attack which he knew had to be a perfect one. He could not afford to let Brack see him any more than he could permit the man to make any kind of outcry.

The banker's own stealthiness helped. He opened the door quietly, sticking his head out just far enough to make a good target. One solid punch rocked him back out of sight and Wayne was after him with a bound, slamming home another blow as insurance, and then dragging the inert man clear of the door. By that time Brack was limp so Wayne took the time to close and lock the door behind him. After that his movements were as deft as they had been on that earlier raid. Chandler Brack was bound and gagged before he could recover consciousness.

Even though Wayne had come with no particular plan in mind he moved with speed and precision. Knowing that Boone Sabbath was due to return soon he appreciated the need for fast work. On the other hand he realized that this job would have to appear as another of El Diablo's lightning thrusts. At the same time he hoped to make more of the effort than a mere nuisance raid.

He dragged Brack behind the bank counter, stowing him into a corner so the banker could get no glimpse of his assailant when he recovered his senses. Then Wayne went boldly into the lighted office, scanning the place for a hint as to his next move. Papers on the desk indicated the nature of the enemy's evening chore. Evidently this was the work which represented Brack's pet secret, so Wayne bundled everything into a big envelope which lay handy. There was no time to read papers now, not with Sabbath due back so promptly. Still the loss of the material would probably be embarrassing to Brack and might even prove valuable to the looter. So Wayne prepared to take them with him.

He smiled wryly at the thought that he had turned to bank robbery. Too bad there wasn't any cash handy; it would be a good collection on account. He considered briefly the chances of forcing Brack to open the safe, but just as quickly decided against it. Too many reasons why that would be a mistake as well as a useless risk.

However — he grinned a little more broadly at the idea — there was a good chance that Brack might be carrying personal funds. Such money would be legitimate booty. He went out into the outer room, closing the office door behind him to avoid being seen from the street, and crossed to where the banker was threshing around angrily, his puffing grunts indicating that he was struggling with his bonds.

"Quiet or I use the foot," Wayne hissed, putting plenty of accent into the words. "El Diablo Negro is merciful if you do not become foolish."

Brack subsided instantly and Wayne smothered a chuckle as he bent over the prone figure to fumble for a money belt. The belt was there, evidently a well-filled one, and the raider unbuckled it swiftly, rolling his man without ceremony as he did so. A grunt indicated the banker's dismay and Wayne smacked him across the ear with an open hand, again ordering silence.

The belt proved recalcitrant, but the delay gave Wayne an idea. Without ceremony he yanked Brack's pants off, slitting the inseams to aid in the removal and not interfere with the ropes on the prisoner's ankles. It seemed like a shame to ruin a good pair of trousers but time was fleeting and Boone Sabbath might just happen to return a few minutes early. When the belt was finally removed from the ruined garment Wayne rolled it up and stuck it into the slack of his shirt, carrying the trousers under one arm as he went back into the lighted office.

There he worked briskly for some thirty seconds, preparing another message in the big, black capitals of El Diablo Negro. After that he needed only another minute in the bank, a minute spent chiefly in dragging Chandler Brack across to the front door. Visions of splinters making their way into the exposed hide of the banker brought another half chuckle to Wayne's lips but he did not speak again, simply depositing his prisoner near the door and leaving it open as he slipped out into the darkness of a tensely silent town.

No one stirred in the immediate vicinity, but Wayne did not delay in getting himself out of sight. He didn't want anyone to ask questions about the big envelope or the slashed trousers he was carrying. All he wanted was for someone other than a Brack henchman to find the town's leading citizen tied up at the door of the bank without any pants on. Brack had practically admitted his own weakness when he showed his anger because people were laughing at him. If that was the tender spot in the enemy's armor Wayne decided that he had thrown a pretty good punch. The ridicule might be even more important than the printed sign which was pinned to the front of Brack's shirt, a sign which read:

"THE BIGGEST THIEF AND MURDERER IN THE TERRITORY IS NOW PARTLY

EXPOSED. SOON EL DIABLO NEGRO
WILL COMPLETE THE EXPOSURE."

Wayne grinned at the thought, circling toward the stable where he had left the anxious Clancy. It took a little time to get there because he headed south for some distance before risking himself in the open to cross the street. Once he made a false start and had to slip back into the shadows to avoid one of Rory Finnegan's patrolling gunnies, but he made the passage safely after that.

Pegleg met him in the shadows beside the stable, the little man's whispered question indicating what the waiting period had done to his nerves. "Did yuh have any trouble, Perry? The town's kinda upset."

"The trouble's all Brack's," Wayne assured him. "Our ornery friend oughta be sweating plenty about now — even if he isn't wearing any pants."

He silenced Clancy's amazed question until they were safely in the stable. Then he told his story, omitting most of the details of the enemy's conference, but outlining the results and making a good yarn of the later events. "And now I'm headin' outa town," he went on. "Keep your eyes open and one of these days I'll be around again, maybe with something else to cram down Brack's ugly throat."

"Take it easy," Clancy advised. "Yuh can't lick him on the first shot, yuh know. Anyway, it looks to me like yuh done a right nice piece o' proddin' fer one day on the job. I'll bet he's fair frothin' at the mouth."

"Not yet. His mouth's too full of his own handkerchief."

"I'd shore admire to see that."

Wayne stopped short. "That's an idea. The thing will have its best effect if somebody besides Boone Sabbath finds him — and Boone is due back there in a few minutes."

"Yuh mean I should wander over and spot him?"

"No. But try to arrange it so that somebody else will. Give me a few minutes to get started out of town, then traipse out into the street. You can pretend to notice that the door of the bank is open, but let somebody else do the finding of our helpless little friend. It'll be safer."

"Jumpin' frogs! But will he be mad! Yuhr neck ain't wuth a busted button from here on."

"No worse than before," Wayne retorted. "Brack made it clear tonight that he wants me killed and not captured. I'm not sure, but I've got a hunch he's not too far off the mark in his guesses about me. So far he hasn't let the rest of his gang know, but I figure he's cagey enough to guess the truth. Anyway, I've got nothing to lose by making him any madder. If I don't win, I'm a dead duck any way you look at it."

He stopped suddenly just as he was starting to slip out into the night. "I've convinced myself," he said, half humorously. "I've got to open the fight a bit. Folks ought to know some of the things Brack don't want 'em to know. That means another sign to be posted. People will kind of expect something along that line."

"Yuh better git outa town," Clancy advised. "Tell me what yuh want and I'll git it made up. Then I kin post it before folks wake up tomorrer mornin'."

"My job," Wayne insisted. "Got a piece of cardboard handy?"

"I'll git some."

He hobbled out of the door, returning promptly with a flat box made of heavy paper material. "From Ben Arms' trash pile," he announced. "Anybody could have got it from there, so it won't put nobody under extra suspicion."

Wayne nodded, frowning a little as he considered the words he ought to use. Then he ripped out a section of the box and went to work with his marking crayon. The result was quite an ambitious message.

CITIZENS OF TINAJA

DO NOT WASTE TIME TRYING TO TRACK EL DIABLO NEGRO. EL DIABLO LEAVES SIGN ONLY WHEN IT PLEASES HIM TO DO SO. BETTER IT IS TO SEARCH FOR THE ANSWERS TO THESE QUESTIONS:

1. WHY DID CHANDLER BRACK HIDE THE BACK OF THE POSTER THAT WAS LEFT IN THE MINERS' BANK?

2. WHY DID NO ONE EVER LEARN THAT JOSHUA LLOYD WAS NOT KILLED BY A FIFTY-EIGHT CALIBER BULLET?

3. HOW DID BRACK GET A SHELL OF THAT CALIBER TO USE FOR A FALSE CLUE WHEN HE MURDERED LLOYD AND FRAMED THE KILLING ON AN IN-NOCENT MAN?

4. WHERE DID BRACK GET THE GOLD TO SALT THE THREE TOES MINE FOR A QUICK SALE AFTER IT STOPPED PRO-DUCING?

EL DIABLO NEGRO KNOWS THE AN-SWERS TO ALL THESE QUESTIONS. IN DUE TIME HE WILL EXPLAIN ANYTHING TINAJA CAN NOT FIND OUT FOR ITSELF.

LET TINAJA MAKE THE EFFORT MEAN-
WHILE.

"That's a hell of a educated line of talk for a Mex outlaw," Clancy criticized. "It don't sound right."

"What's the difference now? All I'm trying to do is to stir up some talk in town, and maybe a few doubts. Now trot along and see what you can do about getting somebody to find Brack. Whoop it up as soon as you can. I'll use the fuss as a cover for getting my end of the chore finished."

"Luck," Clancy said shortly. "Yuh'll shore need it."

10

Wayne waited until Clancy had hobbled off toward the main street, then he worked his own way through another alley and stood in the shadows to watch and listen. Posting a notice tonight was going to be a tough job. This morning he had caught a sleeping town by surprise, but tonight everyone was watching for him. Brack's patrols were along the sidewalks, their very presence doing something to the atmosphere of the place. Even in the stuffy air of a hot evening there was something like a chill of fear.

Clancy was in sight not fifty feet away, idling in a lighted patch where the Palo Duro's illumination relieved the blackness of the street. For several minutes he did not move out of that spot, and Wayne began to suspect that the little man was picking up some of the town's nervousness. Brack's iron control seemed to do that to men. It was one of the worst features Wayne had to buck, and he knew it. He could look for no help unless he convinced honest men that they could turn against Brack without being in fear of their lives.

Suddenly he knew that he had been misjudging Pegleg Clancy. The little man had ignored several passers-by, but now he moved out to take his place beside a lurching citizen who was showing strong signs of drunkenness. There was an exchange of greetings and the two men disappeared from the slash of light. Then, in a few seconds, voices were raised in excitement and Wayne knew that Clancy had done his work neatly enough. He had contrived to have someone else discover that open door of the Miners' Bank.

It did not take long for them to bawl the information to the immediate neighborhood and men poured out into the street from buildings along both sides. In no time at all there was a worried mob converging on the Miners' Bank, every man excited and a little concerned over the safety of the bank, but not one of them willing to enter Chan Brack's building without his consent.

Wayne waited and listened, allowing the stragglers to pass his hiding place before he made any move. It took some little time, but eventually he found the street clear and strode briskly toward the Gem. He would have liked to put his poster on the Palo Duro, but it was too close to that mob in front of the bank. The Gem would do. No one questioned him as he approached and he worked swiftly, big-headed tacks going into soft wood under the pressure of his thumb. Then he circled back through another alley and hurried toward the waiting bay pony.

The noise out front was mounting rapidly as he climbed into the saddle, and a shout of sheer astonishment told him that Chandler Brack had been discovered. Wayne grinned to himself as the roar of astonishment began to turn into something else, something like a murmur of hilarious disbelief. Now Brack's vanity would really have something to fester on!

He took his time as he rode along the back of the main street buildings, trying to avoid any appearance of hurry. It was a fair bet that everyone within hearing of the noise had hastened toward it, but there was no point in taking chances. Those gunmen of Rory Finnegan's might have taken alarm already.

He felt a little twinge of conscience when he sidled past the Valley House. It had been a bit boorish of him not to have sent his

174

apologies by Al Hulett. After all, Moss had tried to be decent, and it wasn't his fault that his invited guest had not been in a position to accept the invitation. Wayne could only hope that Hulett would contrive some sort of reasonable excuse for him. Somewhat less vaguely he hoped the hotel man could square him with the dark-eyed girl — not that it would ever be likely to make any difference.

He had let these thoughts occupy his mind as he pulled away from the main group of buildings, and it was an unpleasant shock when a voice challenged him from the darkness almost at his bronc's nose.

"Who's there?" a man demanded. "Hold up hard, pilgrim! I want a look at yuh."

With the words a light flashed on and Wayne realized that the speaker had been carrying a dark lantern on his saddle. Its rays were aimed squarely at Wayne and the surprise of it made him start. He managed to control himself, however, putting a note of whining complaint into his reply.

"What in fire's goin' on around here?" he protested. "Yuh might think everybody in town was loco."

The guard darkened his lantern again, his voice showing traces of nothing more than curiosity as he asked, "What d'yuh mean, stranger? I heard a bit of a noise in town. What was happenin'?"

"I dunno. I was jest startin' to ride out when some kind of a rowdy-dow broke loose. Sounded like a saloon fight to me."

"Mebbe so. Now what about yuhrself? Where in hell d'yuh think yuh're headed at this time o' night?" Even in the gloom of the open valley Wayne could tell that the lantern was still held in the speaker's left hand while something else bulked in his right. Evidently Finnegan or Boone had interpreted orders a bit liberally and had thrown a cordon of guards around Tinaja, perhaps expecting Diablo to make another attempt to enter the town. At the same time the guards were to examine anyone who tried to leave.

With that in mind he put plenty of whine into his voice as he explained, "Me, I'm gettin' outa this crazy place. It ain't healthy. All day folks have been runnin' around makin' a mighty big fuss over a two-bit outlaw that's runnin' loose in the hills. And all the time they got their bandit right in town. I allow to git myself outa range before they start findin' him roostin' right on their doorsills."

"What do you mean by that?" The question was sharper this time.

"I mean there was a polecat snoopin' around the corner o' the Gem Saloon jest a few minutes ago. I almost run into him before I seen him. All to once I was lookin' into the muzzle of a dam' big gun. It was right then and there that I decided to hit the trail outa town. Me, I ain't no hand fer guns."

"When was this?"

"About ten minutes ago — mebbe twelve."

"Did yuh git a look at him?"

"More'n I wanted. He was a ornery lookin' Mex, I know that much. Even in the shadders I could see the face under the black hat and I thought I'd run smack bang into the devil hisself. Looked jest like the pitchers."

The guard's exclamation was cut off abruptly as a gunshot sounded from town. It served to dramatize Wayne's hastily contrived story, but it didn't have the effect he wanted. The other man edged his bronc a little closer. "Turn around, pilgrim," he ordered. "Yuh're goin' back with me till we find out what kind of a sandy yuh might be runnin'. Mebbe yuh're all right and mebbe yuh ain't. Hustle it up! This is a gun what's aimed at yuhr belly."

It was a bitter blow. Good planning and bold execution were to be nullified by the

177

stubbornness of a single hired gun. Wayne knew that it would be fatal to go back now. Being brought in as a suspect he would be subjected to close scrutiny and would almost certainly be recognized. The very best he could hope for would be a beating at the orders of the vengeful Rory Finnegan.

Desperate danger called for desperate measures, so Wayne made his play without hesitation. The guard had crowded in a little, trying to back up his orders with a show of physical force, and Wayne took the long chance. He pulled the bay horse around suddenly, coming stirrup to stirrup with the gunman and lunging hard for the man's throat. He felt the heat of the dark lantern for just an instant, then his fingers shut off the guard's startled yell of alarm.

At the same moment Wayne felt himself being torn from the saddle. He was crashing to the ground in a maelstrom of vicious blows but he kept his grip on the bewhiskered throat, even when the hard-packed earth nearly knocked the wind out of him. A pistol barrel laid open the side of his head but he scarcely knew it. He was fighting for his life, holding doggedly to the enemy's windpipe and trying to keep the other man from bringing his gun to bear.

He took several punishing smashes from that flailing gun barrel but then he caught the wrist that held the weapon. With both hands occupied he could not protect his face from the left hand of the enemy but he took the punishment and held on grimly, rolling over and over with his threshing opponent in a battle which had to end in death for one or the other. Once he felt heat against his leg and even in the fury of conflict he realized what had happened. At the first attack the Brack gunman had dropped his lantern and the hot metal must have seared both ponies as it fell between them. Both horses had bucked, sending the struggling men to the ground.

A savage fist between the eyes almost made Wayne lose his grip then, but he forced his head close in against the enemy's chest, trying to block the worst of the attack with an elbow. The gunman quickly altered his tactics. The hand which had been beating into Wayne's face suddenly started to claw at the choking hand.

It was an admission of vulnerability and Wayne made his own countermove. For just an instant the gunman was neglecting his gun hand, and Wayne changed his grip on the wrist, twisting hard. He felt the weapon fall against him and then both of them were rolling again, fumbling for the gun, rolling again and always lashing out with knees, elbows and fists.

Wayne knew that he was taking a fearsome beating, having only one hand free to use for defense while his enemy was pounding at him with two. Still he held on, knowing that his very life depended upon that grip on the enemy's throat. He had to maintain the hold, no matter what it entailed.

Then the strategy began to pay off. The blows weakened a little as the other man struggled for breath, then it was a direct battle at the throat of the enemy, Wayne trying to maintain his grip while the desperate gunman tried to pry those tight fingers loose. Wayne knew that a man was dying in his hands but he knew no pity, nothing but a fierce determination to hold on. Hired killers deserved no sympathy — and certainly couldn't expect any in such a spot. It was kill or be killed.

A threshing knee to the groin made Wayne sick, and for a moment he feared that he would lose consciousness. The other man seemed to sense the opportunity for he struggled all the harder, gouging away at Wayne's grip with fingers that tore flesh. Wayne steeled himself, fighting the blackness as well as the enemy, and kept his grip.

Another minute would do it.

The minute seemed like years and Wayne never did know when the fight ended. He simply realized that he was lying across the body of a dead man and that his fingers were cramped on a lifeless throat. He had a dim understanding that he had lost consciousness but he could not be sure. It all seemed like some grotesque nightmare, and he took a moment or two to clear his head before attempting any kind of move.

Finally he pulled his hand away from the throat of the dead man, flexing his cramped fingers until they began to feel like a part of his body again. Then he drew his knees up under him and pushed himself away from the body of the dead enemy. The move made his head swim and he suddenly realized that there was a lot of blood on the side of his face. Another effort brought him to his feet, and he swayed drunkenly and almost fell flat once more. There was a dull ache in the pit of his stomach and he had a feeling that there was not a square inch of flesh on his body which didn't bear some sort of bruise.

For a minute or two he just stood there trying to think. And that was painful also. The distant rumble of excited voices reminded him that Tinaja was in an uproar and that Brack's men would soon be staging a careful search for the man who had outraged their employer. This was no time to be caught in the vicinity of town, particularly with a dead henchman nearby. Discovery by a Brack partisan now would definitely be fatal. He knew that he had to get away fast, but he was afoot and practically helpless.

He tried to whistle for his pony but the effort was useless. His mouth had been cut by the blows which had been driven into his face and no sound would come, only renewed pain. Girding himself to the task he took a few stumbling steps in the direction of what sounded like the restless movement of a horse, but the move was too much for his reeling senses. The lights of Tinaja swirled in his vision and then went out completely.

Pegleg Clancy had done a shrewd job at the bank. Not only had he arranged to let someone else discover the open door of the building but he had faded promptly into the background as the first men came running to the scene. The excited, and none too sober, discoverer had been quite willing to accept his moment of prominence and it gave Clancy the opportunity to observe a lot of details that he would have missed had he remained in the center of action.

The crowd gathered quickly, hesitating for a few minutes and then surging forward as Ben Arms and another man brought lanterns. A dozen men tried to crowd into the bank, only to be halted by a sight which they promptly explained to the less fortunate citizens behind them. Momentary astonishment over the helpless form of Chandler Brack was quickly succeeded by grim glee at his pantless condition. Men might fear the power of Brack, but that was all the more reason why they could appreciate the comic indignity which had been thrust upon him. When it was determined that the bank had not been robbed there was a general tendency to relax and let hilarity have full sway. There is nothing quite so funny as self-importance becoming the butt of ridicule and Tinaja enjoyed the moment to its full. Even as men wondered what other exposure El Diablo Negro had in mind they simply laughed.

Clancy kept his own enjoyment within bounds, watching everything with careful eyes. Some men were laughing guardedly, almost worriedly, as though they feared to be caught at it. Others were unhampered in their merriment. For the moment they were letting themselves go, exposing a dislike of Brack which ordinarily they kept carefully hidden. Clancy tried to remember these men; it might be well to know who was who in Tinaja before long.

Brack was bellowing angry orders in no time at all. He practically drove his rescuers from the bank, his efforts seconded by gunmen who pushed through the crowd as soon as the alarm went out. Their unconcealed menace put a quick damper on the hilarity, and within a very few minutes the bank's door was bolted and the crowd was left to disperse. Clancy noted that Kline, Sabbath, Finnegan and Catfish Smith remained in the building with Brack, while the rest of the hirelings remained on the street to watch outside developments. It pointed up a fact which he had not discounted for a moment. Brack still ruled Tinaja in ruthless, efficient fashion. Even at a time like this he could take over and dominate the situation. It made him a tough hombre to buck.

The laughter subsided quickly as men realized that Brack gunhawks were among them, watching grimly. No one wanted to mark himself for the enmity of Chandler Brack, and the crowd melted away silently. It was at that moment that a new shout of

184

excitement arose. Someone had discovered the sign on the front of the Gem.

Once more Clancy took his post at the edge of the crowd, listening for reactions as a burly man read the poster to the crowd. This time there was a grimmer excitement in the babble of voices. What was this Diablo jasper trying to do? Did he really have something on Brack? Many men seemed to hope so, but the general air was one of disbelief. It had to be another bit of craziness like the morning's performance.

There was no time to think about it. A tall, wiry Circle D man jammed his way through the crowd and snatched the poster from the fellow who had been reading it. This time there was opposition. The big man reached for his gun.

Even as the crowd gave way there was the boom of a single shot. Brack's gunnie was much too fast for the other man. He drew fast, the skill and smoothness of much practice in his actions. Before the big man could get his gun out of its holster he was dead, a forty-five slug knocking him into the arms of men who had not been able to get away quickly enough.

There were warning growls from other Brack men on the fringes of the crowd while the man who had done the shooting swung his gun to cover the angry citizens closest to him. "Anybody else?" he grated.

No one even moved. Tinaja might be ready to laugh at Chandler Brack's mishaps, but the town was not ready for anything more than that. Brack was still boss.

Clancy was bitter as he slipped back into the shadows at the side of the Palo Duro. There had been a lot of satisfaction in seeing the discomfiture of the man who had injured him so sorely, and there had been even greater pleasure in spotting signs of unrest, but the disappointment was even greater. He could not hope for any real support yet. Brack was still too strong, his gang too well organized, and the people of Tinaja still too much in awe of the power which had just been so ruthlessly displayed. Wayne was going to be up against a tough hand; he would have to win his fight singlehanded before he could expect any help. Which would then be no help at all.

Nearly an hour passed and the light still gleamed in the bank building. Brack's council of war was evidently a serious one, the silent knots of men along the street serving as a constant reminder that everyone expected something to happen when the meeting broke up. No one left the street except for an occasional trip to a bar, but everywhere the talk was subdued. After that shooting in front of the Gem no one was willing to start anything.

The patrols were still in evidence but Clancy noted that the gunmen were working in pairs now, their show of force evidently intended to intimidate and at the same time avoid any risks.

Then came the real sensation of the evening. A Brack rider galloped in from the south end of town, passing a hasty word to a couple of his fellow gunmen before going on to the bank. Clancy saw him only as he flashed through a shaft of light from a saloon window, but the glimpse was enough to be disheartening. The man was carrying a ragged Stetson and a strip torn from the front of a tan shirt. Clancy recognized the articles even in the semi-darkness. Perry Wayne had been wearing them when he left Tinaja.

The fellow came out of the bank quickly enough, mounting once more and riding back down the street with a couple of other men who had come to meet him. Everywhere men watched in dull silence, wondering what this new move meant. In another quarter hour they knew a little more, and Clancy began to feel somewhat better. The Brack riders returned then, a spare horse bearing the body of a gunman who had evidently been the loser in a terrific brawl. They halted in front of the bank, speaking to no one, and presently Marshal Abe Kline came out. "Take him to my office," he ordered shortly.

The nervous-appearing lawman hesitated for an instant, then strode along in the wake of the men with their gory burden. His voice was a little shrill as he tried to speak casually to the nearest group of curious onlookers. "Diablo's gone hawg-wild, boys. Be a meetin' at the Palo Duro in about fifteen minutes. Brack wants everybody to be there."

It was an order and everyone knew it, particularly when other Brack men began to pass the word along. Pegleg understood the implications and faded around to the rear, entering the saloon from the back door. It would give him a better vantage point from which to witness the proceedings and at the same time place him in a natural position as an employee of the place. That would be better than appearing as part of an increasingly hostile crowd. He had to play the game as safely as possible until he could find out what had happened to Perry Wayne.

11

Chandler Brack appeared at the Palo Duro almost before the tense crowd was fully assembled. Clad in a freshly pressed pair of trousers and backed by Kline and Finnegan, he came in confidently enough, his heavy face expressionless as he forced his way through the crowd without speaking.

The silence was almost painful as he put himself in a commanding position at the end of the long bar. Not only was his audience too curious to waste time with comments but they were all too aware of the gunmen who had taken their posts at strategic spots throughout the room. No one knew what sort of attitude Brack would take, but it was clear that he was making a show of force. Tinaja was warned that there was to be no monkey business about this meeting.

Then Brack smiled. It was a pretty good smile, all things considered, and the audience relaxed a little. They weren't fooled by it but they still felt the lifting of a burden. Brack was going to play it in his regular manner. He was going to be smart rather than tough, keeping the silent threat of violence as his ace in the hole.

"Men," he began calmly, "there have been some mighty odd things happening in this town today, things which have been a deliberate attack upon me and upon my reputation." He let the smile come again as he added, "And I don't mean the childish prank of stealing my pants."

There was a general chuckle and Clancy grimaced. That had been a smart comment on Brack's part. He was giving his hearers a chance to laugh at him even though he hated the idea, letting himself become the butt of good-natured humor instead of the other kind. It established him as a friend of the men he addressed and paved the way for whatever he planned to say to them. Maybe that was the reason Brack had been so successful in all his schemes; he knew how to turn every trick to his own account.

"We've been invaded," he went on more seriously, "by an outlaw whose early performance seemed too crazy to be explainable. It was only in the light of his later acts that his game began to make sense. That's why I asked you men to come here now. It's time you knew the facts."

He had their interest, even to the point where they were forgetting those gunmen on their flanks. The room was deathly silent as Brack continued, "In the first place there is no such person as El Diablo Negro. Some of you know that already. The real Diablo was killed nearly two years ago. Our mysterious outlaw simply adopted the disguise because he wanted to stir up trouble in Tinaja without exposing his own true identity. The Diablo getup was striking enough so that anyone who saw him would remember him, and forget his real characteristics. We'll have to admit he succeeded at first. We didn't understand the meaning of his actions then, and he sure did get the attention he wanted."

There was a murmur of partial understanding and then another flat silence. The crowd was almost with him and Brack hurried on, forcing home his reasoning with a certain amount of earnestness. He would drive the people of Tinaja if he had to, but just now he was trying to win them over.

"We can be certain that the morning's appearance was our outlaw's method of calling attention to the Diablo character, in order that he might turn up later in a different disguise, just as a stage magician makes cute passes with his right hand so the audience won't spot what he's doing with his left. Diablo was with us all afternoon and nobody recognized him."

Again there was a stir of interest, but Brack's voice rose enough to carry over it. "Tonight it all became quite clear when he killed a Circle D rider — only after my man put up a brave battle. Circumstances which are too detailed for the present discussion tell us the identity of the outlaw and also the disguise he used on his second trip into Tinaja. He is a dangerous criminal, an outlaw with a price on his head — a price which seems to have made him desperate to the point of being foolhardy. His plan was to catch your attention and to make ridiculous charges against me after being sure that his first crazy stunts would guarantee your attention to the charges. He hoped I would buy him off rather than let his statements get that attention.

"His raid against my home was a part of his campaign to get attention, but his visit to town this afternoon was to let me know his real demands. It was a bold strike and, as you can well imagine, he gave me a bad time. However, he was just a little too bold for his own good because now we know a few things about him. The important one is that he was here in town during the afternoon acting like a saddle bum. He is about six feet tall, has black hair and is clean shaven after getting rid of the Diablo disguise. He was riding a bay horse with four white feet. Some of you remember him, I'm sure. He's the man who slugged Rory Finnegan right out in front of this place."

There was a murmur of comprehension and Finnegan rubbed his jaw reminiscently, glowering at the men who turned grins in his direction. Brack went on hastily, "He killed Frazee in making his getaway, but I don't believe he knows that he has been recognized. That's the point we must use in catching him. If he doubles back into town again I'm depending on you men to take care of him. And don't be careless! He's just crazy enough to be deadly."

His face hardened perceptibly as he added, "I mean just that, men. Kill him on sight if you want to save your own skins. My best information is that there are rewards totaling a couple of thousand dollars on his head, and no lawman appears to be particular about getting him alive. I'll add a thousand to whatever else is offered."

"Alive or dead?" someone called from the rear.

193

Brack smiled. It was not a pleasant smile. "What do you think, Maguire? If some polecat had clubbed you over the head, swiped your pants, and told lies about you, would you be fussy? I just want to get rid of the dirty scoundrel before he can think up any more fantastic lies to tell about me."

Again there was a murmur of understanding. Brack knew how to play his cards. No one had even questioned the shooting of that man in the street. Pegleg had been wondering whether anyone would, but was not particularly disappointed when no mention was made of the incident. After all, there wasn't a thing to be blamed on Brack there. The dead man had gone for his gun first and Brack would be certain to point out that fact.

All things considered Clancy was badly worried when he stumped away to his quarters in the stable. Not only had Brack displayed his brains in seeing through the business of the disguise, but he had pulled a real master stroke in telling the town his story, with its variations. What had appeared to be a tight hole for him had been turned to a probable advantage. There had been just enough truth in his yarn for it to fit the known facts. Now people would believe him and might follow his open suggestion about killing the raider on sight.

Clancy also was worried over the fact that Perry Wayne would have no way of knowing about this new turn of events. Wayne would feel reasonably safe in his secondary disguise, but actually it would mean almost certain death for him to meet any of the gunmen who would be out looking for him in his present character. Clancy even considered the chances of searching for Wayne in the Sierra Verdes, but he quickly abandoned the idea. His own physical infirmities were too great for the large amount of riding which almost certainly would be necessary. All he could do was to be ready in case something turned up in Tinaja.

What bothered him even more than that was the clear evidence that Wayne had engaged in a bitter struggle with that dead gunman. Evidently he had gotten clear away but he must have suffered a lot of damage, judging by the way the shirt had been torn and the way the dead man carried marks of a brawl. It was even possible that Wayne was so badly injured as to be helpless out there in the valley. But where? Clancy spent a thoroughly uncomfortable night thinking about it.

It was dark. Not a peaceful sort of a dark

but an uneasy blackness in which fear and pain chased each other through the shadows. And there was noise also, a noise which brought dread even to dulled senses. It required several minutes for Wayne to get his wits about him but then he remembered his plight and knew that he had been unconscious for some time. The pains he had known in his semi-conscious dreams had been his own, while those noises were the sounds of approaching horsemen. That was why his dulled brain had tried to make him aware of danger.

He did not trust himself to rise but crawled hastily in the direction of the Sierra Verdes. That would take him away from the dead man and also out of the path of the oncoming riders. He could hear them talking now and knew that his first guess had been correct. Two Brack riders were out searching for the missing guard.

"He oughta be right around here," one of them growled. "Funny we don't hear him movin' around none."

The other man laughed, shortly and with a trace of nerves. "Mebbe that spooky Diablo run off with him."

"Shut up! This ain't no time fer jokes. I don't like the looks o' things."

Wayne inched his way into some taller

grass, aware that the two riders were beginning to circle, evidently beating the country where the missing man had been posted. He hoped he could keep clear until they should locate the dead man. Not that the diversion would be of any permanent good. It would simply be the signal for a full scale hunt.

He held his breath as a horse clopped past him, but then came the astonished curse of discovery. "Here's Ed!" a voice yelled, shrilling in its excitement. "Git over here and look at him. He's been beat plumb to hell."

"Dead?" the other rider called, spurring away from Wayne.

"Dam' right." They conferred in low tones over the body but Wayne made no effort to catch the lowered voices. He was crawling again, trying to put distance between himself and the two men behind him. Presently there was the sound of a flurry of hoofbeats and he knew that a horse was being spurred hard for Tinaja. Now it was going to be awkward. One man was riding in to give the alarm while the other remained with the body.

His knees were worn through by that time, but he still continued to crawl, inching along toward the hills. Behind him there was an occasional creak of leather as the lone rider shifted nervously in his saddle, but there was no hint that he had heard anything of the crawling figure to the west of him.

Wayne lost account of time and distance. He knew that he ached in every bone but he plugged doggedly onward. Twice he almost lost consciousness but kept going, forcing himself to move even though he scarcely knew why. It came as quite a surprise when he finally heard a distant shout behind him. It was the lone rider shouting to guide the approach of other horsemen coming out of Tinaja. For a moment Wayne simply lay flat on the ground, resting and listening. He could not believe that he had come so far, but it was certain that those voices were quite far away — enough to make it safe for him to get up and walk, if he could make it.

He tried. A dozen painful steps brought the dizziness again and this time he crumpled in a heap without even realizing that consciousness was leaving him.

When he opened his eyes again it was still dark but the chill of morning had come upon the valley. There was even dew. He rubbed his eyes, discovering that his face was still mighty sore and that his hair was wet. It brought the truth back to him and he guessed quickly that he was still some distance short of the hills, and daylight was approaching.

He listened carefully but could hear no sounds of riders so he worked himself to his feet again, taking precautions this time. He still had plenty of sore places but his head was clear now. Maybe he could make the hills afoot before daylight.

He was just beginning to feel safe when there came the sound of something moving behind him. He stopped to listen and heard the noise again, more distinctly this time. A horseman was stalking him from the rear, riding easily and with frequent stops.

Wayne drew his gun as he stared into the darkness. He vowed that one man would not take him back, not after all he had gone through. It would have to be a fight, but he was ready for it.

The unseen trailer came again, moving just long enough for Wayne to spot his general position, then he halted again as though to listen. Wayne tried to guess at distance but held himself tense and ready.

The thud of hoofs sounded once more, quite close this time, and suddenly Wayne glimpsed a silhouette against the stars. Almost afraid to believe his eyes he called softly, "Come on, Cottonfoot. Come on, boy."

The bay horse snorted a little and came toward him, tossing his head as Wayne reached for the bridle. There was a vast relief in the man's tones as he patted the pony's neck and talked in a husky whisper. "Been followin' me, have you? Good boy. Now we'll get somewhere."

It took an effort for him to mount, but his spirits were rising now and he even felt a little less battered as he turned the bronc's head toward the north. The trail would be longer that way but he knew that trackers would be out at daylight. He had to lead them astray if he hoped to have any sort of security in his hideout.

Daybreak was reddening behind him when he worked into the low hills west of the Circle D buildings. By that time his head was clear and he ventured to make enough of a detour to have a look at the ranch house. No one seemed to be stirring there, so he assumed that Brack had not come out from Tinaja. Then he rode straight into the hills, making sure that he used cattle trails or the various other routes which had been well marked up by the riders of the previous afternoon. Finally he swung into the brook and repeated his ride of the previous morning. He was groggy when he finally arrived at the hidden glen but he was reasonably content. It would take a tracker with a sixth sense to follow him here.

Darkness was dropping swiftly across the mountains when he awoke from the exhausted sleep which had followed the ride. He moved his battered limbs painfully, finally forcing himself into action. Having no knowledge of the enemy's position he did not dare risk a fire, so he contented himself with some cold food and a long drink of cold water. After that he felt well enough to take some heed to his physical condition. A decent shirt and his regular Stetson would make some difference in his appearance when next he ventured abroad, but he would have to take that risk. Somewhere out there in the valley he had lost the old battered sombrero and most of his shirt front.

First, however, he attended to his injuries, using cold water as a cure-all. Aside from the badly scraped knees and the dig on the side of his head there were no open wounds, and he decided that he had not suffered any really serious injury. A good bath did wonders for him and he lay down again feeling ready for the next round, whatever that might bring.

This time his sleep was more normal, and when he opened his eyes to starry skies he was ready for action once more. The stars told him that it was about three o'clock in the morning so he climbed out of his blankets, a little stiff and sore, but anxious to get on the move again.

He even risked a fire, guarding the blaze with due care long enough to boil some coffee and heat up a can of beans he had taken from the Brack stores. After that he saddled the bay and slipped out through the cedars.

Dawn was reddening over the Javelinas across the basin when he worked his way out into the lower foothills just west of the Circle D buildings. He did not take the risk of moving into his old observation post, contenting himself with a more distant spot on a commanding hill. He arrived there with the first real daylight, just in time to see four riders pulling up at the Circle D corral.

"Brack, Dimmick, Finnegan and Catfish Smith," he murmured aloud. "I wonder what's on their program for today?"

Turk came out to help Smith take care of the horses, and the other three men disappeared into the house. Turk and Catfish followed as soon as they had done their chore. Wayne wished that it might have been dark so that he could do another piece of eavesdropping. It had been a lucky move last night, and he had a hunch that this morning's meeting would be equally enlightening.

The sun rose higher, clearing the Javelinas and sweeping the valley clean of its gray shadows. Then the back door of the ranch house opened and a slender figure emerged. It was the blonde girl Wayne had left tied up on his previous raid — probably the girl Vicara Moss had referred to as Jan. She was dressed in what he guessed was an Easterner's idea of correct riding garb, but she went alone to the stable, evidently able to take care of the saddling chore without help. Which seemed a little odd to Wayne. Turk wasn't such a valuable man at a conference that he could not have been spared to take care of such a chore for the boss' new lady.

Wayne prepared to leave his observation post but the girl did not come toward him. Instead she rode away in the direction of the spur of hills which jutted out into the valley some distance north of Circle D. He watched her thoughtfully, only turning back to his study of the house when she disappeared behind the first ridge. It was clear that she was not a very experienced rider, and he wondered that she should venture into rough country alone.

The waiting became irksome after a time. The men in the house seemed to be in no hurry to make a move and Wayne was on the point of departing when the whole crew came out into the open once more. Again Turk and Smith took care of the corral chores, saddling fresh animals. Apparently some sort of lengthy movement was on the program.

There was a conference beside the corral after Brack, Dimmick, Smith and Finnegan were mounted. Brack seemed to be outlining some sort of plan and his gestures toward the west and southwest hinted that his words had to do with the trail of El Diablo Negro. Evidently he proposed to make a new attempt at tracking the troublesome one, this time with a little more care and with fewer followers to ruin sign.

Wayne did not wait for them to start out. He hurried back to his bronc and climbed gingerly into the saddle, still quite aware of his many aches and pains. He had not planned on being cut off like this and he didn't want to provide a fresh set of tracks for these enemies.

Even as he turned the bay and started back into the deeper hills he realized that he could not afford to lead the searchers toward the hidden glen. One way or another he had to make his tracks in some other direction. Accordingly he turned off at once, striking northward on a course that would take him squarely across the path of the quartet he had been watching. It was a bold move, but there was an element of safety in it. He knew he could cross their trail before they could reach the point of intersection, and he had a feeling that he might even do it without having them detect the move. They would not be paying much attention to sign yet but would have their minds occupied with thoughts of picking up the trail which the posse had lost two days before.

He put the bay to a gallop, soon crossing the little valley which he figured Brack and his men would use. He took a little time there, masking his crossing hastily and then sending the bay forward at a run when he was into the hills north of the intersection. Just in case his crossing was noticed he wanted to have a head start.

A mile or so to the north he circled sharply and climbed a ridge which he knew would give him a commanding view of the rolling country through which he had just ridden. For some minutes he scanned the undulating greens and browns below him, seeing nothing resembling a moving figure. Then a tiny haze of dust caught his attention and he studied the trees in that direction, soon spotting the four riders who were working their way back into the more rugged country.

So far so good. They had not even noticed the new sign, he thought. Maybe he could even do a little trailing on his own account now, watching for an opportunity to confuse them by leaving sign which they would spot on their return. He wheeled his bronc, preparing to drop back down into the lower country, and was startled to find a blonde girl in a tweed riding outfit not fifty feet away. She was studying him quizzically from beneath the brim of a big hat that seemed a trifle too large for her, her glance carrying a trace of interest which was even more pronounced than the mild alarm which she was trying to hide.

He covered his start with the skill of much recent practice. "Howdy," he drawled, riding directly toward her. "I didn't hear yuh comin'." He hoped there would be no trace of El Diablo Negro in his voice.

"I was already here," she told him flatly.

He frowned, then asked, "Yuh mean yuh been watchin' them?" The jerk of the head indicated the riders far to the south.

"I was. Any reason why I shouldn't?"

"I reckon not, ma'am. It jest seemed a mite strange."

"I felt that way about it when I saw you doing the same thing. Odd that we should both be so interested." Her glance had been a sweeping one, taking in the details of both man and horse. He had an uneasy feeling that she was seeing more than she ought to, but there was nothing in her tone to indicate a suspicion. Wayne forced himself to think hard. He had to pretend that he knew nothing about her, hoping that she would take him for a complete stranger. At the same time he wondered why she had been spying on Brack. Probably jealous over something, he decided.

"I didn't know anybody but me was interested," he said finally, replying to her comment without committing himself.

"Well, I am," she said, her tone indicating that she was done with pretense. "And I quite understand that you are. I saw your haste to get here and I have a feeling that you've been doing some spying from a closer distance."

He tried her own line on her. "Any reason why not?"

"Not to my knowledge. But aren't we wasting time sparring like this?"

"Yuh're talkin' riddles, ma'am. I don't know a thing about yuh and I ain't even started to guess why yuh're watchin' Chan Brack. Fer all I know mebbe yuh're his gal friend and yuh figger mebbe he's sneakin' off into the hills with some other piece o' calico."

She flushed a little but her eyes were steady as they stared into his. "That's the second time in three days that a man has jumped to the conclusion that I am intimate with Mr. Brack. The other time I didn't bother to deny it. This time I do."

"I'll take yuhr word fer it," he said, trying to sound disinterested while he wondered what she meant by telling him so much. "I was jest jokin'."

She came back to the point. "I'd still like to know why you were spying."

"Yeah? So yuh could tell him all about it, I suppose?"

"Don't be a fool. I think there's something mighty peculiar about that man — and I think you're of the same opinion. That's why I'm talking to you like this. You're the first person I've met who even hinted that he might be on opposite sides from the important Mr. Brack."

"Yuh ain't baitin' me into nothin', sister," he growled. "Jest 'cause yuh're a right purty gal ain't no reason fer a man to git hisself fouled up with Chan Brack. That jasper throws a heap o' weight in this part o' the country."

Her expression was impossible to interpret. For just a second she stared at him, then she swung her pony away and rode into the trees, not even looking back. Wayne watched her until she disappeared on the pine-clad slope, then he turned his own mount toward the west and dropped down into the valley to circle back toward the part of the hills where Brack and his crew had gone. That blonde girl could be plenty dangerous. Either she was being mighty smart in her effort to make him betray himself or she really wanted help. In the latter case she had plenty of troubles of her own and Wayne knew that he was in no position to assume any more than had already come his way. In the future he would try to make sure that he didn't get tangled up with the girl. She could turn out to be real poison.

12

Wayne frowned unhappily as he cut around the hillock and started for the broken country where he had last seen Brack and his men. With a ticklish scouting problem ahead of him he knew that he ought to get his mind free of any distracting matters but memory of the blonde girl's eyes kept bothering him. They were rather attractive eyes, but it was the expression in them that he recalled. She had seemed hurt by his words but at the same time she had betrayed something like stubbornness. He was almost ready to doubt his own conclusions about her. Maybe she was all he had thought, all Clinton Moss had hinted, but she might have turned out to be a good ally.

Just as quickly he blamed himself for even thinking such foolishness. This was no game for a woman, particularly one like that blonde. Regardless of what her real intentions might be she was dangerous. He simply couldn't afford to take any extra chances.

He rode swiftly but easily through the hills, aiming to cut the trail which he had used on the previous day and which now seemed to be the center of attention for Brack's outfit. It seemed sure that Brack had something in mind connected with that trail and Wayne could not guess whether the renewed interest was the result of a new idea on Brack's part or merely an added urge for vengeance. Suddenly he remembered the papers which were still rolled up in his slicker, papers he had all but forgotten in the frantic activity of the past thirty-six hours. Maybe that was the answer. Brack was making an all-out effort to recover those papers.

He was tempted to hole up somewhere and look over the documents, but he decided against it. For the present he needed to keep a closer watch on Brack and there was no certainty that the papers were as important as he imagined. Better to let them wait another few hours.

He found the trail of the enemy without difficulty and knew that the four men had been ambling along at a pretty good pace through this part of the hills. Evidently they were concerned only with the country ahead, the rolling country where El Diablo's trail had vanished.

Wayne still played it safe. He did not propose to gallop into any kind of ambush if he could help it so he kept the bay at a walk, studying the trail even as he kept an alert eye on the terrain ahead. It seemed likely that the hunters would spread out when they reached the brook where El Diablo had started his evasion tactics. From that point one or more of them might double back, and Wayne didn't propose to blunder into a meeting just yet.

He was within a half mile of the brook when he heard the unmistakable clink of a shod hoof striking stone. Instantly he swung the bay aside, taking cover in a pinon thicket that was convenient. Even as he did so he heard the sound again and knew that it had come from somewhere in his rear.

He pulled his six gun promptly and a little grimly. So that was the game, was it? Brack and his boys had been bait to draw him out of hiding. The real hunters were the rear guard who were now closing in. It puzzled him that he had detected no sign of such a second force around Circle D, but he did not let the perplexity interfere with the grimness of his intentions. He was going to be up against a tough game; now was as

212

good a time as any to start a real fight.

Another clink of iron on stone told him that the pursuer was getting close, the now distinct hoofbeats indicating a lone rider who was taking no particular precautions against discovery. Maybe this wasn't going to be so tight after all. He peered out through the pinons and uttered a perfectly audible "Damn" as he spurred the bay back into the open. The rider coming up the valley trail was the blonde girl in the big hat.

She flinched a little at his sudden appearance, but pulled up her pony without any outcry. From a distance of about ten feet she studied him with the same troubled look in the blue eyes.

"Look, sister," Wayne growled, making his voice as unpleasant as possible. "This is no cute little game we're playin' out here this mornin'. If yuh're as innocent as yuh make out to be yuh'd better make tracks outa here before some slugs begin to fly. If yuh're as nosey as I suspect yuh o' bein' yuh better make them tracks before I git plumb sore. Either way, git!"

The stubborn light was in her eyes as she returned his glare. He had a feeling that she had reached some decision and was about to declare herself.

Her words were completely calm, however,

as she asked, "Why do you suspect me? I've already given you more than a hint that I'm on your side of the fence."

"Who said I was on any side?"

"I'm not blind."

"And I'm not dumb! It's hardly likely that Chan Brack's newest fancy lady will be selling him out at this stage of the romance. Yuh ain't had time to find out what a polecat he is."

A faint flush suffused her cheeks, but she kept her voice as steady as ever. "I slapped the last man who made a suggestion like that."

Wayne's hand started toward his cheek but he caught himself quickly. Not quickly enough, though. The girl smiled thinly. "I was almost sure of it before. The hazel eyes, you know. Now I'm certain. Are you ready to talk sense?"

He tried to outstare her, but made a poor job of it. She seemed to have gained confidence in herself, even though the worry was still clear in her eyes.

"It's you who's makin' the crazy talk," he told her, giving up the battle of glances.

"Let's not hedge. You're the man who treated me so roughly when you were pretending to be a Mexican outlaw. Now let me tell you a few things. I came to this country because I began to suspect that Chandler Brack had cheated me out of some property. His letters were smooth enough, but I smelled a rat. When I arrived in Tinaja he was most hospitable, insisting that I come to his home as his guest, under the proper chaperonage of his housekeeper."

She paused as Wayne smiled broadly. "That was the part you were so ungallant as to misinterpret. And I see you still don't believe me."

"I'm almost beginning to," he informed her. "I just got a laugh outa Mamie Rook bein' a chaperone. She's —"

"Anyway, I accepted the invitation for what it seemed, but very quickly came to the conclusion that he was simply keeping me away from the town, probably because he didn't want me to learn something or other which I might have heard about there."

Wayne nodded, silently and a little uncomfortably. The girl's manner made it impossible to disbelieve her, and he was acutely conscious of the insulting remarks he had made. More to cover his own confusion than for any other reason he asked, "How long have you been there?"

She smiled again as she replied, "Since the day before you appeared on the scene.

And I'm glad to notice that you're abandoning that ridiculous drawl. It was a little too thick for belief. I think you did the Diablo act better."

"You're a cool hand," he conceded, matching her amused smile. "Go on with the yarn. It almost could be true."

"It is true. I was getting up my nerve to leave the ranch house and start for Tinaja when you popped in. By the time I got over being scared pink I was too helpless to do anything. It was only after you had gone that I realized that I had missed a good chance. An opportunity to talk with Brack's enemy might have helped me."

"Sorry I had to get rough," he apologized. "I didn't —"

"I'm not blaming you too much. The few hours of discomfort were worth while because they helped my thinking. I saw that I was in something of a trap, and I was even more sure of it when those men came hunting for you that afternoon. Brack was badly flustered by what he found in his room, and he was very particular about keeping me from being seen by any of those men. I even read the message on the mirror, although Brack doesn't suspect that I did."

"But my game is no part of yours. You can turn to the law for help. I can't."

"I'm afraid the law won't be of much good to me. Brack seems to own whatever law this country has. I have a feeling that a partnership between us will be much more efficient. I'm sure I need help — and I think you do, too."

"What makes you think I can't handle my end of it?"

"I've heard talk at the house. He is already aware of your double identity. That much I heard before those men practically drove me out of the house this morning. They know definitely that the man who posed as El Diablo Negro is now riding around the country on a white-footed bay horse. They know he is wearing ragged clothing and acting like a hobo. They know he is clean shaven, has black hair and is about six feet tall. They also know that he bears numerous cuts and bruises. That's how I happened to recognize you back there on the ridge. I let you insult me out of it for a minute or two, but then I decided to follow you and have an understanding."

Wayne could almost feel his lower jaw dropping. Someone had betrayed him. It made him a little sick to think that Pegleg Clancy had played him false, but he knew that it was a possibility. Even if Hulett had let the cat out of the bag by talking too much to those Eastern people there wouldn't have been quite so much information in Brack's hands.

"How did they get so smart?" he asked, trying for an answer he was not expecting to hear.

"I don't know. I just heard talk, you know, but I'm of the opinion that they were pretty sure of themselves."

He started to ask another question, but before he could frame the words there was a cry of alarm from the girl. He saw that she was staring toward a patch of woodland just beyond the pinon grove, in the direction toward which he had been heading before the interruption. He reacted instantly, flinging himself from the saddle even before her frantic "Look out!" was fairly spoken.

The flat bang of a six gun came with the vicious whine of a slug, but by that time Wayne was afoot, his own gun in his fist as he looked across the bay pony's back. There was another exclamation from the girl and two shots boomed almost in unison, the bushwhacker getting in another hurried blast as Wayne fired more deliberately, and heard a resulting scream.

"Are you all right, sis?" Wayne asked, quickly glancing around to make sure that she had not been struck by either slug. "Then hold my horse a minute."

Without waiting to make sure that she would obey orders, he ran across to the prone body of the man he had cut down with such deadly precision. It was the Brack gunhawk known as Catfish Smith. He was dead, one efficient forty-five slug having drilled him an inch to the left of the breastbone. One glance was enough for Wayne and he hurried back, reloading the one used chamber of his gun as he did so.

"Time to get out of here," he announced, taking the bay's reins from the girl and climbing into the saddle. "That shot will bring company, I suppose."

He could see the horror in her eyes as she stared past him toward the dead man, so he spoke harshly, urgently. "Stop gawking and get that nag on the back trail. Hustle it up! And try to keep on the same lot o' tracks you made when you rode out here. The more we can confuse them the better chance we've got to live."

The goading tone had its effect and she obeyed orders, seeming to forget the sudden death she had just witnessed. It was only for a minute, however, and presently she turned her head to ask, "Was he dead?"

"Yep."

There was a distant shout from the hills behind them and Wayne listened carefully, trying to guess where the rest of Brack's crew must be. He believed that they were trying to locate the sound of the shooting. So far, at least, they had not started any pursuit.

"I'm glad." It was the girl, and for a moment he wondered what she was talking about. Then he realized that she was continuing the other topic, evidently trying to talk away her own sense of horror at what she had seen. He let it go at that. She would have to steel herself for worse than that if she proposed to try tricks on Chandler Brack. The man would be beaten only by violence, and it was just as well to get the shooting started now.

There was no more talk until they reached the point where Wayne had come down from the northern hills to cut Brack's westbound sign. There he snapped a crisp order: "Swing left and ride up that draw."

She obeyed without hesitation although she seemed to realize that they were no longer headed toward the Circle D. A glance at the ground told Wayne that he and the girl had been the only ones on this trail recently, so he called a quick halt, speaking a little grimly as he pulled up to sit stirrup to stirrup with her. "You can take it alone from here, sis. Try to find some of the tracks you made when you first rode into the hills. Muddle things up all you can and then swing out into the valley at some point north of that spur of hills. After that go straight back to the house."

"But what are you planning to do?"

"I'm not entirely sure. It's a cinch they'll raise a loud hullabaloo over Smith's death, and I suppose they'll use it as a point against me — maybe as a means of stirring up a lynch mob. One way or another you want to keep clear. If you're lucky maybe they won't get wise that you were on hand."

"But no one saw you shoot Smith, or whatever his name was," she protested. "How can they — ?"

"Precious little difference that will make. Anything off color gets laid to my door from now on. Brack will see to that. All I can do is to make sure that I give 'em plenty to blame me for."

"Won't you be in terrible danger?"

"I am already. But what I'm trying to do isn't exactly a sewing circle proposition. Now get along with you before somebody spots us. If anything turns up that you need to get in touch with me again you might try riding over to the spot where we ran into each other first, when we were both watching Brack. I'll try to get around to that part of the country along in mid-morning tomorrow or next day. Don't try to go there if you are being watched, and don't take any chances if you can avoid it. Your life won't be worth beans if that crew even suspects you've been talking to me."

"You'll be there tomorrow?"

"I'll try, but don't depend on it."

"But isn't there something I can be doing to help?"

"Sure. You can be keeping your eyes and ears open, and you can be playing so dumb that they won't try to get rid of you. That's your big risk; if they suspect you, it'll be fatal."

"I'll be careful."

"That's the best plan, unless you get really smart and duck away like I suggested before. You can try the law, you know. It might be a lot easier than what I'm trying to do."

Her question hinted that she had paid absolutely no attention to his advice. "Are you a friend of this man Wayne that I heard Brack talking about?"

"In a way. I'm on his side."

"Good. I had a notion he'd be all right and would make a good friend."

"Get going," he told her shortly. "Remember what I said." He swung away before she could continue the conversation. It was going to be important that she should not be detected by the Brack crowd. With her on the inside he might gain certain advantages which he could not hope to acquire while playing a lone hand.

He was thinking hard about the whole arrangement as he cut back, fouling the sign as much as possible to protect the girl against detection. He went as far as he dared, then swung away, not caring to risk another armed clash with the men who must now be on his trail. He had been pretty lucky in that brief but deadly battle with Catfish Smith, and he didn't propose to crowd his luck too far.

He put the bay to a steep climb, emerging on a shoulder of the mountain where he could look down into the tangled valleys where he had recently been riding. He caught sight of men almost immediately and slipped back into cover, picketing the pony and returning to a sheltered observation post. Brack, Finnegan and Kline were down there, riding slowly along in single file toward the open valley and the Circle D. Finnegan was leading a bronc which carried the body of Catfish Smith.

Wayne muttered grimly. Two men killed in two days! He had known that this would result in violence, but the actuality was still a little hard to take. Even though the victims had been killers well deserving of the fate, it was not pleasant to think of what had happened. Nor was it any better to consider what would probably happen in the future. This skirmish would certainly be used by Brack to put his enemy on the wrong side of the law. Presently otherwise honest citizens would be riding in Brack's train, ready to shoot down the "outlaw" who had murdered Catfish Smith. That was the way Brack would make it work out — and Perry Wayne would be faced with the necessity of fighting with men he wanted as his friends.

What was even more troubling, when he took the time to think about it, was the way Smith had fired without warning, practically from ambush and in the presence of a witness. It indicated that the girl had been telling the truth when she reported overhearing the part about Brack's men seeing through the change of disguise. Smith's shot had settled the matter. The man had recognized Wayne and had shot to kill. It meant that any new attempt to enter Tinaja would have to be postponed indefinitely.

Wayne's battered features were more than

a little haggard as he went back to his bronc and started across the mountain's hunched side, aiming for a long, irregular slope which would lead down into the broken country to the south. He had never been under any illusions as to the perilous nature of the task he had set for himself, but it was disheartening to build up hopes and then have them dashed. He had been counting pretty heavily on the help of Pegleg Clancy, and it hurt to know that the little man had played traitor. Somehow he felt that it was that way. Hulett and the Mosses had not known enough to be too dangerous; it must have been Clancy who had let the cat out of the bag.

"Can't make the same mistake twice, Cottonfoot," he said aloud to the bay pony. "We won't give that tow-headed gal a chance to do any tricks. Maybe she's all right and maybe she ain't." Then he added half whimsically, "Never trust a woman. The poetry books are just full of horrible examples."

The pony's ears flicked as though he understood and Wayne chuckled, the by-play relieving his feelings a little even if bantering talk could do nothing for the various aches which still plagued his body.

He worked his way toward his hideout, using the brooks and ledges as he had taught himself to do, finally coming out at a point along the main ledge which led to the cedar brake. There he pulled up and dismounted, leaving the bay once more while he went down the slope afoot to examine the tracks of Brack's searching party. A little study told him that the enemy had not even come close to unraveling the puzzle he had set them, so he climbed back again, feeling a little more cheerful even though the effort was making sore muscles ache most uncomfortably. Maybe he was playing a lone hand against nasty odds but he still had a card or two in reserve. Sooner or later there ought to be a break in the right direction.

It was well past noon when he found himself in the glen once more, his trail neatly erased and both horses grazing peacefully. Only then did he surrender to his weariness and discomfort. He took the time to attend to his injuries, still sticking to the cold water cure, then he crawled into the hut and wrapped a blanket around him. His mind told him that he ought to lose no more time in looking at those papers he had taken from Brack's office, but weary flesh argued the other side of the issue. Weariness won. That was one of the big disadvantages of riding the outlaw trail. A man never could make a decision without having some part of it forced upon him.

13

Again Wayne more than slept the clock around, waking to find streaks of dawn filtering down through the overhanging cedar boughs. He slid out of his blankets, sloshed his face swiftly in the brook by the cliff, and decided that the lost hours had been worth while. The dig on the side of his head was still tender but the other scrapes and bruises were practically forgotten. A hasty look at the nearby country told him that no one had been prowling around while he slept, so he put together a hasty breakfast, even building a tiny fire of deadwood for heating coffee and some more of Chan Brack's airtights. He hoped that the telltale smoke would be lost in the morning mists, but he was willing to take the risk. Many an hour might pass before he could have another cooking fire and he wanted to start the campaign with a little heat under his belt. It helped.

He dressed without thought of disguise, putting his saddle on the black horse. Since the connection between El Diablo and the saddle bum was already known there was no point in adhering to fine distinctions between characters.

He wondered idly about the last query the blonde girl had tossed at him. Evidently she did not suspect that the raider was Perry Wayne, only that Wayne was interested. Did it mean that Brack was equally ignorant? Or was it simply that the girl had not heard it straight? He decided that it didn't make much difference. Regardless of name he was bullet bait for any gunhawk who could get him in his sights.

The rising sun hit him squarely in the eyes as he moved down across the ledges so he dismounted promptly, leading the black where the timber offered shelter. He could not afford to make any rash moves now; always he must know what was ahead.

Suddenly he had an idea, one of those flashes that come from nowhere, bringing complete disgust that the point had not been understood before. Of course Brack did not know that Diablo and the saddle bum were Perry Wayne! Otherwise there would have been a concentrated search around the old Wayne ranch. Brack would have realized that the fugitive would be working in familiar country, not dodging around on a lot of spiraling ledges.

It was just as clear that neither Clancy nor Hulett had been a traitor. Either would have told all. So Brack was simply guessing, probably from the evidence of the hat and the piece of shirt left back there beside the dead gunman.

The morning seemed suddenly brighter. It was good to know that Clancy had not betrayed him. Maybe matters were not as hopeless as they had seemed. There were still friends in Tinaja.

He smiled thinly at his own elation. Precious little he had to get enthusiastic about! Up to now he had made himself a nuisance to Chandler Brack and he had killed a couple of hired gunnies, but nothing real had been accomplished. He still didn't know how he was going to put over any sort of attack that would be of permanent value to him.

His mind seemed to be awakening all over. The saddle roll with the papers in it! Maybe those papers held the answer! He had thought about them during the past afternoon, but he had been too busy or too tired to examine them. This morning he simply hadn't remembered.

He halted, about to turn back, but second thought told him that the matter would keep. The immediate need was to scout the enemy. A man couldn't take time out now when the opponent might be closing in for a kill. He had to know what Brack was doing this morning. Papers could come later.

He paused to read sign at the spot where Catfish Smith had died in his bushwhacking attempt, then he left the trail of the other Brack riders and swung directly east, approaching the Circle D buildings from the south in order to avoid beaten paths and the disadvantage of looking into the sun. It was sound tactics for presently he caught the glint of something flashing. Working carefully into a better position he studied the spot again until he caught the glint and a dark movement behind it. A rifleman was posted on a ridge directly behind Circle D. The trap was set!

He swung westward again without hesitation, using every trick in the bag as he worked into the higher hills. It took an hour to do a couple of miles, but he crossed the old trail without discovery and made his way to the previous day's vantage point. From there he could see Circle D apparently deserted. Probably everyone was lying low, waiting for him to make the rash step which would explode in bushwhack gunfire.

A further scout to the north indicated no one on the ridge where he had agreed to meet the girl. A couple of hours of waiting made it clear that she was not going to appear. He would have to go right on making guesses. It left him with a sense of disquiet but he thought he understood. Brack was playing a cat-and-mouse game, counting on superior position to trap a rash enemy. So far as Brack knew, Wayne would still be depending on the false security of the saddle bum disguise and might walk into the trap.

Thought of it made Wayne shiver a little. He might have made that very fatal error if he had not been warned. It was one thing he owed to the blonde girl, no matter how troublesome she might turn out to be in the future.

He returned to the glen by the same cautious route he had used on the previous day, keeping an alert watch even though he did a lot of thinking. It seemed certain that he had guessed Brack's strategy correctly. The theory also accounted for the girl's absence from the foothills. She was probably being kept at the ranch house, either because she was already under suspicion or simply because Brack was taking no chances on anything interfering with his trap. Wayne tried to tell himself that it was the latter.

Back in the glen he went straight to the business of the papers he had taken from Brack's desk. They were confusing as well as enlightening. Some of them were ordinary legal documents dealing with transfers of real estate, all of them seeming to be perfectly legitimate even though there was included the foreclosure papers on his own ranch. Brack had made everything legal, even though the schemes behind some of the transfers were probably no more ethical than the Wayne fraud.

The rest of the collection was more of a muddle. A pair of letters brought unexpected confirmation of the girl's story about herself. One letter, evidently the first, was a simple request for information, signed by Janice Knight. Wayne remembered that Vicara Moss had referred to her missing friend as Jan, so he concluded that his guess had been correct. The blonde girl at Brack's was the one the Mosses were trying to locate. That part of his guessing had been correct, even though he had done the girl a grave injustice in assuming too much with regard to her reason for being at Circle D.

The thought was quickly lost beneath a new interest as he read the letter. It was in neat feminine handwriting and stated that the writer was searching for facts regarding the estate of Joshua Lloyd, deceased. She hinted that she had expected some sort of inheritance, but offered no information as to a possible relationship to Lloyd. That put a different face on matters. So the blonde girl was interested in the Lloyd matter, was she? That put her right in the middle of the whole business.

The second letter was more specific and was in reply to something Brack must have written in answer to the first one. This time she specified that she was Josh Lloyd's niece, and that he had written her some months before telling her of his gold discovery and promising that it would be hers upon his death. She seemed to be quite troubled by what Brack must have written and her underlying doubts were quite clear.

Wayne could guess at the rest, knowing these few facts in addition to what the girl had already told him. She had simply written for information at first and had been given a reply which aroused her suspicions. Accordingly, she had come out here to learn a few things at first hand, and Brack had made one of his usual smart moves to keep her from learning about whatever swindle he had perpetrated.

Finally Wayne turned to the rest of the

papers he had scooped from the desk. Most of them seemed to be just scratch paper. Several sheets were literally covered with a peculiar crabbed handwriting, looking like something a child might have done in practicing penmanship. Single words were repeated over and over, while on one page there was nothing but single letters drawn and redrawn in that same cramped script. Always the letters were ragged and irregular, the sort of letters an illiterate person might have traced out without any knowledge of their meaning. So far as Wayne could determine they were not the work of any writer he had ever known. Nor did the practiced words make too much sense to him. One page was taken up with just five words, all of them repeated many times. They were *partner, understood, owner, absolute* and *it.* On another page the same writing had produced a few phrases like *the said Chandler Brack, shall make no assignment* and *to have and to hold.* It was the phrases containing Brack's name which had been written the greatest number of times.

He remained in the glen until late afternoon, pondering the possibilities of the papers. So far as he could make out there was just one good reason for their existence, and he was almost afraid to believe in it.

Although he could see no immediate way of using them he had a definite feeling that here was the legal evidence which had been eluding him for so long. For the first time he had something which could be used against Brack in a court. Now all he had to do was to find some way of getting to that court alive. And it wasn't going to be easy.

An hour before dusk he saddled the black horse again and slipped out into the hills, working cautiously toward the valley before making the swing north to flank Circle D. It meant more painstaking travel since he had to guard against traps. Brack wouldn't continue his waiting game forever — not with those incriminating papers in the hands of his enemy.

This time his scouting expedition told him that the baited trap was to be continued during the night so he went back to the glen once more, grudgingly content with the stalemate. The delay might force Brack's hand, but it was still a strong hand. Brack held all the big cards and now he was fully alert to his own danger.

He was in position on top of a commanding knoll when the first rosy hues of dawn began to silhouette the jagged peaks of the Javelinas. As the glow reddened into daylight he saw signs of activity around the distant buildings. A man left the ranch house and rode away toward Tinaja. Five minutes later Turk and the blonde girl came out and strolled across to the corral. The surly one roped a horse for her and saddled it, standing back while she rode away up the valley to the north.

Wayne considered the move a little perplexedly, but it did not require many minutes to bring him an explanation. The girl had scarcely disappeared from view when three men bustled out of the back door and ran to the corral. They saddled swiftly and rode hard toward the hills. Their immediate direction was westerly, but Wayne could see them even after they entered the first fringe of rough country and he knew that they were heading north, trailing the girl from the protection of the ridges.

Then two men carrying rifles came out, proceeding directly into the hills west of the ranch. The guards were being placed once more. Evidently Brack had a hunch about the girl, but he was not banking too strongly on it. He was going to play the hand for all it was worth.

For a minute or two Wayne considered the merits of making a circle to intercept the girl, but then he decided against it. There was only risk involved, and nothing to be gained. He didn't think that she would be in any danger so it seemed best to keep entirely clear of the obvious trap.

Still it was maddening to do nothing but wait. Her move hinted that she had information, and it was distinctly annoying to sit tight here on the hill and pass up the chance of getting whatever she could offer.

Hours passed and he still waited, chafing at the necessity, but forcing himself into inaction because it seemed like the only logical choice. Then, when he was almost ready to do something foolish out of sheer impatience, he saw four riders breaking out of a wooded draw some distance north of the ranch. Conree and Janice Knight rode ahead, the other two Brack men loafing along in the rear. At a glance it seemed like a peaceful little group, but Wayne knew better than to accept it as such. Even at the distance he could detect a tension in the girl's attitude, a hint of fear covered by careful dignity. She was being brought back to Circle D under guard, virtually a prisoner, and she knew it.

He watched until she was taken into the house, two of her captors remaining outside as guards. After that there was another lull, broken only when Conree and another man rode out toward the near hills. They were gone only a matter of minutes, returning with the two riflemen who had been posted there.

That seemed a bit odd. They were unsetting the trap. Did it mean that the girl had fooled them with some story or other? Or were they switching tactics? Or were they simply offering a possible watcher a feeling of false security in preliminary to a swift attack? If it should turn out to be the latter, Wayne decided that he would not be fooled. No matter how tedious, he would have to stick it out and watch.

14

Somehow he managed to endure the laggard hours. The sun's angle told him that it was well into the afternoon when finally there was a new show of activity below him. Conree and two other men mounted horses and slipped away in the direction of Tinaja, while a third man struck out across the prairie into the northeast. Meanwhile Turk brought two saddled ponies from the corral, leaving them saddled by the door of the house.

Then there was another hour in which Wayne had nothing to do but to worry about the plight in which Janice Knight must be finding herself. Still there was nothing to be done, so he went right on with the tedious waiting.

The break came when Brack and Sabbath appeared, mounting the ready horses and speaking a few words to Turk as they went away from the house. Turk promptly disappeared from view.

It occurred to Wayne that here was the same situation as on the morning of his first raid. The house had the same three occupants. Maybe it was a good hunch to play. A swift raid now might pay off. It would be a long shot, but the game was getting desperate now; he would have to take chances.

Then came a move which caught him completely by surprise. Turk came out of the house almost at a run and went straight to the corral. He saddled two broncs and took them back to the house just as the bulky figure of Mamie Rook appeared on the back stoop. There was a bit of broad comedy as Turk heaved the fat woman into a saddle, and then the two conferred at some length. After that Turk rode straight toward the hill which had once served Wayne as cover for his observations of the house. Mamie followed at a little distance, evidently bawling some sort of instructions to her dull-witted helpmeet.

The big man disappeared from Wayne's view for only about five minutes, then reappeared to ride directly back to Mamie. Again there was a bit of serious talk, and the pair went into the house leaving the ponies at the back door while they went into the building.

"The king's horses and the king's men," Wayne muttered aloud in his perplexity. "Rode to the hill and rode back again. What in thunder was the meaning of that crazy little *pasear?*"

By that time he knew that he was not ready to make any hasty move. Something mighty queer was happening down at the Circle D, and he wanted to see more before staking his own play on any part of the situation.

More minutes dragged by while he waited impatiently, his mind wrestling with the puzzle. Certainly Turk could have gone no great distance into the hills and it was clear that he had not returned because of any omission. Mamie's waiting attitude had been quite obvious. The whole thing had been planned that way. But why? It had hardly seemed worth all the effort of hoisting the big woman into a saddle.

The next move brought understanding. Turk and Mamie appeared once more, hauling a helpless third figure between them. Wayne knew that it was the blonde girl, and her clumsy movements indicated that she was bound. She was being practically carried between the other two and they lifted her bodily to throw her across the back of the bronc Turk had been riding.

Then the comedy was repeated, Turk heaving mightily to get Mamie up on the other horse. Then he climbed into his own saddle, shifting the girl's body so that he could handle the extra burden. Wayne had a grim suspicion that the girl was unconscious or dead, but he did not let his mind dwell on the subject. He had to watch this deal and plan to make some sort of countermove.

Once more there was a sharp bit of conversation, Mamie doing the talking. Her rapid gestures hinted that she was trying to drive something into the thick skull of her brutish husband, while his impatient nods indicated that he wanted to reassure her as to his complete understanding. Finally they seemed to reach an agreement and both of them rode away in opposite directions, Mamie taking the trail to Tinaja while Turk with his helpless burden started for the hills.

Wayne couldn't afford to delay any longer. A grim suspicion had already entered his mind and his lips were set in hard anger as he sent his bronc down the slope in a direction which would permit him to cut the trail he hoped Turk was going to take. Only briefly did he consider the chance that he might be running into an ambush. He had seen no additional Brack forces in the hills, and his estimate of the new move told him that there would be none. Anyway he was in no mood to consider the risk. He had to intercept Turk before the man could get very far from the open valley, just in case it was not already too late.

The bay had plenty of speed and in spite of the distance he had covered during the early hours he was still fresh, the slow pace of the early travel and the long rest having given him plenty of chance to conserve his abundant energy. The crashing descent was a matter of seconds, and then the pony was running hard through a series of wooded draws which ran parallel to the open valley, angling presently westward so as to gain distance for a cutoff. Wayne could only hope that he was guessing correctly. Otherwise —

He knew that he was ahead of Turk when he reached the gulch through which Brack and his men had ridden on their earlier search. Now he had to gamble. If Turk was moving in some other direction it was just too bad.

He dismounted quickly, leaving the bay loose with reins dangling. Then he started back along the rough trail, keeping to the brush and moving as noiselessly as possible.

He had not covered a hundred yards when he heard hoofbeats ahead of him, the slow, measured thud of a heavily burdened horse. Taking cover behind a pine he watched and saw Turk moving directly toward him, the girl a limp gray burden across the horse's neck. The first glance told him that Janice Knight was still alive, but there was scant consolation in the knowledge. Turk was staring nervously about him as he let the pony climb the easy grade, and it was clear that he was ready for trouble. Both the uneasy glances and the cocked gun were evidences of the big fellow's nervousness, and the worst part was the way that gun bored into the helpless girl's back. It was a powerful argument against interference.

Wayne knew a feeling of utter despair. Even a bushwhack bullet might prove fatal to the prisoner. Turk's whole bearing made it clear that her life would be forfeit in the event of an attack — and he was just low enough in the scale of animal life to have a reptile's tenacity of existence. Even if hit fatally he could probably squeeze the trigger.

Still Wayne knew that he had to take the chance. The girl was being brought into the hills for just one purpose — a purpose which had to be balked now or not at all. He waited, almost fearing to breathe as he steadied himself for the shot which had to

244

be absolutely perfect. Once he saw the surly man's eyes pass right over him, but there was no sign of understanding. Turk came on doggedly, his ugly face completely expressionless, only the narrowed eyes showing signs of life as he glanced around him. Then he was abreast of Wayne and the time had come for the move that would mean everything.

Wayne knew better than to be overcautious. He drew fine on his target and fired quickly, fearing that any attempt to delay the shot would produce a tension that would defeat the whole purpose. There was a bellow of rage and pain from Turk as Wayne's slug drove the gun from a shattered hand, then frenzied action developed along several lines at the same time. The startled bronc bolted, throwing both Turk and the girl to the ground. Wayne could not even risk a glance to see whether the girl had been injured by the fall. He had to move fast for Turk was already scrambling for a second gun, clawing for the weapon with his good hand. Evidently the instructions hammered into his stupid brain by Mamie had been well clinched. He had a job to do and he was going to do it.

Wayne bounded forward, but he was too late to block the big man's frantic movement. Turk had already rolled to his knees and was swinging his extra gun into action, not toward the man who had ambushed him, but toward the inert form of the helpless girl. One idea at a time in his thick head was all he could handle. His job had been to murder the prisoner and he proposed to do it if he could.

Wayne fired again, hastily but with a calm viciousness which made him wonder at himself. Twice he put slugs into the lumbering killer, placing them with a grim deadliness in which there was no vestige of pity or compunction. Turk was a mad dog to be exterminated, and there was no pleasant way of doing it.

The first shot spoiled the big man's aim, his bullet plowing dirt some distance beyond the prostrate girl. The second one stopped him dead. His heavy jaw dropped in an expression that was vacantly comic, then he collapsed in a heap, not even a grunt coming from his slack lips as his body hit the ground.

Wayne took no chances. Without even glancing at the girl, he jumped across to pick up the gun which Turk had dropped, for good measure also scooping up the dented weapon which had been the target of his opening blast. Then he stirred the

246

dead man's hulking carcass with a boot toe, satisfying himself that the dirty job was actually done. Then without a backward look he went across to cut the thongs which bound the girl's arms to her sides.

She stirred a little as he rolled her over, but did not regain consciousness. Feeling a little awkward he examined her hastily, searching for broken bones, and was pleased to find nothing seriously wrong. Her hair was hanging loose, and the gray dress was torn and rumpled, but she was breathing evenly and there was a spot of color in her cheeks. It brought him a quick sense of relief, particularly when she did not regain consciousness while he was making the examination.

He stood erect again, suddenly aware of other dangers which he had been forgetting. Twice he whistled, a low quavering note which was calculated to travel a limited distance. Almost with the sound the bay horse ambled into view along the trail, coming obediently at the signal.

"Lucky I had you along, Cottonfoot," Wayne said aloud. "That fancy black rascal never would learn to recognize my whistlin' ability."

The bay approached gingerly, tossing his head as though aware of the dangling reins

247

which usually were his cue to remain quiet. Wayne reached out to relieve him of the worry, patting the unkempt neck with an approving hand. "Good boy. Now you get rewarded by having an extra load to carry. Sure, I'm a mean critter, but it can't be helped. We've got no time to catch that Circle D bronc, so you're elected."

He stooped to pick up the girl in his arms, lifting her to the saddle and steadying her there while he climbed up to hold her erect in front of him. "Let's go, hawss," he directed. "This ain't no time to be standin' around with your teeth in your mouth. Maybe Turk wasn't as much alone as he was supposed to seem."

The bay turned at his nudge, moving away at a good pace toward the deeper thickets of the upland country. Wayne let the reins drop across the arm which held the girl, pulling his six gun once more and holding it ready. A man never went too far wrong to keep a weapon in hand at a time like this.

Darkness was just beginning to settle over the broken country at the foot of the Sierra Verdes when Janice Knight opened her eyes and groaned a little. At the first sight of movement Wayne tightened his arm around her, and it was well that he did. Consciousness seemed to return abruptly after that first sound of distress, and she began to struggle with desperate earnestness.

"Take it easy," he advised, keeping his voice calm even though he was having to hold her tightly. "We're in a fair way to be all right. Don't make me spill you overboard."

She subsided abruptly, turning her head to stare at him in astonishment. Then, suddenly, she laughed. There was a trace of hysteria in the nervous little giggle, but there was humor as well. "Spill me overboard," she echoed. "That's not the kind of language you were using the other day." Before he could frame a reply, she went on with the sort of question he would have expected to come first. "What happened? How did I get here?"

"Never mind about it now. Just relax and give yourself a chance to recover."

"What do you mean recover? What happened to me?"

He smiled, partly to reassure her and partly because he admired the quick show of returning spirit. At least he was not going to play nursemaid for a panicky woman. "I'm not sure that anything serious happened," he told her. "All I know is that you were unconscious, but I don't know whether you fainted or were knocked cold by falling off a horse. One way or another you can stand a bit of rest, so take it easy."

She shook her head as though to clear it. "I'm all right, I think, aside from a few odd sore places. I guess I must have fainted." Something like horror slipped into her voice as she almost whispered, "What happened to that beast? Turk, I mean."

"He won't bother you again."

She looked him squarely in the eyes. "I understand," she said flatly. "And thanks."

"Can you sit in the saddle now?"

"I think so. But I don't want to make you walk."

"I'd prefer it that way. From here on we've got to hide our tracks and in this gathering darkness I don't want the bronc to stray into any place where sign will show. We'll be safer if I lead him."

"You're the boss. I'll take care of myself well enough."

He slid to the ground, easing her back into the saddle as he left it. There was a moment of hesitation as she tried to adjust herself to the unfamiliar gear, then Wayne suggested, "Just sit sideways. The bronc will be walking and you won't need to worry about stirrups."

She accepted the advice without comment, neither of them speaking again until

250

they halted before the screen of cedars. Then he touched her knee in the darkness. "Come on down. This is where everybody has to walk."

She let herself drop into his arms, speaking quickly and with a trace of agitation as he steadied her for just a moment. "Could I ask where you're taking me?"

"Sure. To the outlaw's den. That's the story Brack will tell, I suppose, and he won't be far wrong."

"It's no joke," she half whispered. "He proposed to tell something almost like that."

"We'll swap yarns in a few minutes," he promised. "Now get a good grip on the bronc's tail and follow along behind him. Look out that a tree branch doesn't spring back and hit you in the eye. We're going through."

He led the bay past her and started into the thicket. "Got hold?" he called back.

"I'm with you."

"Good girl." He meant it just that way. The break in the situation had not been what he might have wished for, but he could be thankful that he had not run afoul of one of those women who collapse or become hysterical in moments of stress. Maybe this girl was a bit too headstrong to suit the tastes of Clinton Moss, but she was not a

251

bad sort for this kind of a jam. In spite of the rough time she had experienced during the past few hours she was holding up well.

It was pitch black under the cliff when they broke out of the cedars, only a few stars blinking down from the narrow strip of sky that was visible. "Hold it right there," he told her. "Sit down and rest if you want to. I'll unsaddle the pony, and we'll hold our confab."

She was still standing quietly when he smacked the bronc playfully across the rump and sent him toward the brook which flanked the cliff. "Over this way," he directed. "Sorry my hospitality can't be any more genteel."

She reached out to take his arm, holding it lightly as he guided her toward the unseen shack. He knew that her hand was trembling a little, but she kept her voice well under control as she replied, "No apologies necessary. I didn't come visiting in what you might call a very formal manner."

"Sit here," he suggested. "I'll take a chance on a fire long enough to make some coffee and heat up a quick snack. We both need it, and I've got a hunch there won't be anyone around to spot the fire just yet."

"We'll be safe until midnight," she told him quietly.

"How do you know that?" He asked the question as he built his cooking fire from the carefully selected materials already collected for the purpose.

"I heard the whole thing planned." Again there was that sternly repressed note of horror in her voice.

"Want to talk about it? Don't if you'd rather not."

"I'll talk. The telling won't make it any worse, and you ought to know."

"Very well. Skip the part about them following you to the ridge this morning. I watched that and I knew you were going back to the house as a prisoner. Just go on from there."

253

15

She did not speak until he had his fire going and a coffee pot simmering on the carefully built little blaze. Once he glanced at her to make sure that she had not suffered from some sort of reaction, but she gave him a half smile which reassured him. Seeing her thus in the firelight, the blonde hair still tumbling in disarray and the torn gray gown tattered and twisted, it occurred to him that she was a remarkable young woman in many respects. Not only had she kept her emotional control under the worst kind of conditions, but she still contrived to look attractive through it all.

She seemed to understand what was going through his mind for she took up her story with suspicious haste. "Mr. Brack was at the house when they took me in this morning — he and three other men that I did not know. At first he simply tried to question me about where I had been, but when I refused to answer he locked me in my room. I knew I was in a dangerous spot and the only thing I could think of was to try a bold bluff. I changed from my riding clothes to this dress, hoping to put on a show of dignity which might scare him into letting me go." There was bitterness in her little laugh as she added, "I guess I didn't know him very well. Eastern clothing didn't impress him even a little bit."

"Then he didn't bother you much at first?"

"No. That came later. When he let me out of the room the other men were gone, and he tried to be very smart, telling me that he was doing it all for my own good, that the man I had tried to meet was the murderer of my uncle."

"Then you are Janice Knight, niece of Josh Lloyd?"

"Yes."

"I'm Wayne. The man accused of killing him."

"But you didn't do it." The statement was as calm as the other exchanges of information.

"Of course not."

"I believe you. Anyway, I let my anger get the better of me, and I accused Brack. I knew from what I had seen on the mirror that you believed him to be the real murderer. So I let him think it was my own idea that he had done the thing and had pinned the crime on you. It fitted perfectly with the scheme for stealing the mine, as I was beginning to see it."

"Let me guess about that," Wayne cut in, trying to slow her down and keep her from becoming too excited. "He had shown you a paper by which Lloyd's share of the gold mine partnership went entirely to Brack in the event of Lloyd's death. That was his evidence to deprive you of your inheritance, but you knew that it was a forgery. Right?"

"Exactly. How did you know?"

"It seemed likely, although I didn't pick up the point at first. You must have known that your uncle was almost uneducated, that he could barely write his own name."

"Precisely. And the partnership paper Brack showed me was in my uncle's handwriting, or rather a type of writing which looked like his signature. I knew he could not possibly have written it."

"And that's where we've got Brack where we want him — if he gives us a chance to use the information. I found the papers where he had been practicing his stunt of copying your uncle's writing. It was a case of being too thorough. He wanted a document which would give him unquestionable claim to the mine, but he didn't need it until you turned up with a counterclaim. Then he decided that the paper would be more convincing if it was in your uncle's writing. So he worked one out, using a signature as a model for making the various letters, and not knowing that a signature was the only thing Josh Lloyd had ever written. I didn't remember it at first, but when I started to think about the matter I remembered that Lloyd used to get Ben Arms to do his writing for him. It must have been quite a shock to Brack when he discovered that he had been too smart for his own purposes."

"Shocked enough so that he promptly decided to kill me," she retorted. "And I was too smart for my own good, too. I shouldn't have told him how much I knew."

"Better go on with the story," Wayne said after a moment.

"Brack hit me when I told him he was lying. I think he dragged me into my room and locked the door again, but I'm not sure. Either I fainted or the blow knocked me unconscious. Anyway, I woke up on the floor of the bedroom and realized that someone was talking in the next room. It wasn't pleasant to hear. They were planning to kill me and to put the blame on you."

"I thought so. Could you tell who was doing the planning?"

"Brack and another man with a low voice. And Mamie."

"Then the others had left the ranch by that time?"

"I think so. I knew that Brack and the other man were also getting ready to leave, and it was only after they left that I heard the full details. Mamie made them clear when she went over the whole thing for that stupid husband of hers. She was trying to make sure that he wouldn't get mixed up. He was to take me into the hills and murder me, and she was to ride into Tinaja and report that you had come to the house and kidnapped me." Her voice faltered a little as though the memory was too much for her. Then she uttered a short little laugh that was more bitter than mirthful. "I suppose it sounds pretty flat when I tell it that way, but I simply can't describe my feelings at hearing it the way I did. I think I must have really fainted then."

"I don't blame you. But try to get all the details straight. It might be important if we ever get a chance to tell our story to an honest lawman."

"I remember them well enough. I'll never be able to forget. Turk was to shoot me and leave my body at about the same spot where you shot that other man — Smith, I think they called him. Then he was to ride over to a place they called the northwest line camp and stay there for the night. He had to remember that he had been searching the hills for you and had been at the line camp since mid-afternoon. That was the story Mamie tried so hard to drum into his head."

"And Mamie was to report another raid on the house, eh?"

"Yes. She was to ride to Tinaja and tell that you had surprised her and kidnapped me."

"Then the rest is easy. Brack was planning to kill two birds with one stone, if you don't mind the phrase. He wanted to arouse Tinaja citizens to killing anger against me, and he wanted to get rid of you. In that way neither of us would ever have a chance to talk — which is what he had to guard against. It was almost a brilliant scheme."

Neither of them spoke for several minutes. Then it was the girl who said slowly, "Maybe I know too much already, but I'd still be interested in knowing what happened to Turk. I know that I became dizzy when Mamie was giving him his final instructions. I guess I fainted again, but I have a dim memory of being very uncomfortable and knowing that I was slung across a horse like some old blanket roll. I tried to get up and knew that Turk was jamming something into my back and threatening to kill me. Then it all went black again. How did you manage?"

"I was lucky. I shot the gun out of his hand before he could pull the trigger."

"Then you didn't kill him?" She seemed disappointed.

Wayne smiled thinly. "Not with the first shot."

She accepted it that way. "Does his death alter the situation?"

"Not much, I'm afraid. Brack will drum up a frenzied gang of half-drunken citizens, and they'll find Turk's body instead of yours. But that won't bother a fast thinker like Chan Brack. He'll promptly claim that Turk died trying to save you, and the hot chase after me will become hotter than ever."

"But we can ruin the whole dirty scheme now. I can, I mean."

"How?"

"I'll simply go out to meet the posse."

"As easy as that, eh? You're forgetting what a tricky character Brack is. He'll know you're alive when he finds Turk, so he'll push his campaign accordingly. I'd guess that he'll shove his own men into the advance guard and keep everybody else back. They'll have their orders — and the orders will be 'Shoot to kill'."

"Oh." There was more emotion in the single syllable than she had displayed in telling the whole tale. For the first time she seemed to realize the seriousness of the spot they were in.

"Why did you say we'd be safe until midnight?" Wayne asked.

"Because that would be the earliest we could expect a search party in the hills. Mamie wasn't to arrive in Tinaja with her wild story until after dark. They planned to bring men out to the house tonight, ready for the fake search in the morning. So no one could be here before midnight, and I don't think we'll be bothered until tomorrow."

Wayne chuckled as he passed over a tin can of steaming coffee. "You figure smart, sis. Here. Don't cut your lips on the ragged edges. I'll have something a little more solid to go with it in a jiffy."

She almost dropped the hot metal, but recovered to wrap the can in a fold of her dress. "So I figure it all out," she replied quizzically. "What does it mean to us?"

"It means we can make tracks out of here before the posse swings into action."

261

"Where can we go?"

"Oro City. I think we're ready for a move. We know what Brack wants, and we've got some pretty substantial evidence against him — none of which we could use in Tinaja. So we'll switch to Oro City and make just as much loud noise as we can. Maybe we can interest the territorial authorities."

"Can we get to Oro City?"

"I think so. It's a better bet than waiting to meet the crazy mob Brack will have out here at daybreak."

She sipped gingerly at the coffee, apparently paying no attention to anything except the hazards of drinking scalding liquid out of a ragged tin can. Suddenly, however, she asked, "And what about you? My part is clear enough. I can tell my story and produce papers to back me up, particularly if you'll let me have the ones you mentioned. But I don't see that you're in a very easy spot. What will save you from arrest on that old charge?"

"Nothing. All I can do is work to prove that it was a part of a long range program of crookedness on Brack's part."

"Pretty thin for that kind of case, isn't it?"

"Maybe."

"Then we're not going to Oro City."

"Oh yes we are!"

"No."

She met his eyes defiantly across the little circle of firelight. He grinned at her briefly as he said, "Thanks for being a good scout, but there's no point in getting balky. Oro gives us a chance, which is something we won't have here."

"I'm not going to let you take the risk."

"Don't get cocky. You've been toted around the country as a prisoner before, you know. I guess I can do the same thing."

"You wouldn't."

"I will if I have to."

Again there was silence. Then she laughed another of those short, half nervous little giggles and said, "I guess you would, at that. But I know what I'll do. I'll fix up my story so as to tell about overhearing Brack's confession on the old murder case. Since it was my uncle who was killed, they'll be likely to believe me."

"Thanks again, but you didn't overhear any such thing."

"How do you know I didn't?"

"Because I think it was a secret Brack didn't talk about — a secret he kept even from his henchmen."

"But you're only guessing. So I heard it."

He studied her for a long time in the

263

firelight as she put on a good show of being stubborn. Finally she had to look away, and he spoke slowly, only a mild chuckle breaking into the exaggerated drawl which he had used in his secondary disguise. "Lady," he said, "I shore was plenty wrong about yuh the other day. Yuh're a right square shootin' kind o' heifer. Mebbe yuh oughta give me another good slap jest fer good measure."

This time her laugh was a merry one. "I'm trying to forget the incident. And you might call me Jan. That's what my friends call me."

"Then it's Jan. If you ever have to do any slapping in the future it will be for an entirely different reason."

Her reply seemed to come from the depths of the coffee can. "I'll be looking forward to it."

Wayne let it go at that. He was remembering some of the words he had heard spoken by Clinton Moss. Maybe the man had not been too far wrong in one way.

"Better stoke up on some of this slumgullion," he suggested flatly. "You'll need all the strength you can muster before we're done with this night. And I'm talking about the ride to Oro."

She didn't seem to like the note in his voice as he made the last statement. Certainly there was acid in her own tones as she snapped, "I should certainly hope so."

They completed the meal in a somewhat strained silence, the fire dying out as Wayne ceased to feed it. The glen was almost completely black again when he stood up and poured water over the glowing embers.

"Feel better?" he asked, trying to be casual again.

"I'm fine, thanks."

"Then you'd better take forty winks. I'll rout you out in about an hour and we'll hit the trail."

"What about you?"

"I can skip the sleep. In the last couple of nights I've been way ahead of the game."

"How far is it to Oro City?"

"Twenty-five miles, I suppose. Why?"

"It's going to be an awkward ride for me, you know."

Suddenly he understood. The girl was not outfitted for rough riding such as they planned. "I'm sorry," he apologized. "I forgot about the shortage of side saddles in my outfit. Ever ride astride?"

"No."

"Good time to learn. Clothespin style ain't what you'd call real ladylike, but it's a heap better way to handle a pony."

"But this dress —"

"Change it. I've got some duds you can

wear, if you don't feel that you have to be on your dignity."

Again the short laugh was mostly rueful. "It's a little late for that. I seem to have classified myself already. Let's have the clothes."

"I'll have to find 'em first. When I stopped being El Diablo Negro I put the black outfit away in case a snooper happened along."

"Then I'm to be the bandit?"

"Yep. Actually you'll be more comfortable in that garb than in anything else I could produce. Better stuff in the outfit, and it's smaller because it was supposed to be tight for me. You'll have less to lap over."

"Very well."

He moved away in the darkness, fumbling for passage through the brush to the spot where he had cached the black clothing. It took him quite a little time, but when he returned to the spot where a burned odor marked the site of the dead fire she was waiting calmly enough.

"Sorry, no jewelry, mirrors or anything. You'd better climb into these things right away. Then if we have to get out of here in a hurry you'll be ready to ride."

He deposited the bundle beside her and stepped away a few paces. The rustle of cloth indicated that she was getting on with the chore.

"Can you manage?" he asked.

"Yes. Don't strike any matches."

"Don't give me ideas."

She made no reply to that, and he could hear little grunts of annoyance as she fumbled with unfamiliar garments. Finally she spoke aloud, mildly triumphant. "I think I'm fixed," she announced. "All but the boots. They're miles too big."

"Wear your own. The main idea is to be rigged out in pants and shirt to make the ride as comfortable as possible."

"Then I'm ready." —

"Good. You'll find blankets in that little hut right behind you — good blankets from the Circle D. Take what you need and get some rest. You've had a tough day, and will likely have a tougher one ahead of you."

"Right, boss," she agreed, suspiciously meek.

He turned away, walking to where the thump of an occasional hoof marked the position of the grazing ponies. He spoke softly to them, reaching out to touch the nearer animal. The smooth coat was dry, so he knew it was the black. Giving the bronc a pat he moved on, still talking as he started to give the bay horse a brisk rubdown with cedar twigs. "Got to keep you in trim, Cottonfoot," he commented. "You've got a lot o' feet to pick up and lay down."

Jan was breathing softly and regularly when he went back toward the hut so he remained silent, merely pulling a saddle blanket around his shoulders as he stretched out close to the little patch of lingering warmth which told him where the fire had been. In spite of what he had told the girl, he knew that his own efforts of the day had taken something out of him. He was tired, emotionally weary from the strain of waiting and fighting. Maybe forty winks would be good for him. Certainly he wouldn't oversleep; he was too conscious of danger for that.

He still seemed to be thinking along that line when he opened his eyes and knew that he had been sound asleep. He looked up at the sky, searching for a hint as to the hour, and was alarmed to discover that an overcast had obscured the stars. That was bad. It had been bright starlight when he was rubbing the bay horse. It must have taken some little time for those clouds to develop.

He reached out a hand toward the fire site and found only dampness where he had poured the water. The ashes were cold.

Instantly he dropped the saddle blanket and clambered to his feet, calling softly as he took a couple of quick strides toward the hut, "Jan. Wake up. We've overslept."

There was a little groan and then a rustle of cloth as the sleeper sat up. "What? Oh, now I remember. Are we ready to start?"

"We're late. I fell asleep and didn't wake up."

"What time is it?"

"I don't know. Can't see the stars. How do you feel?"

"Awful."

"You mean you can't travel?"

"I don't mean anything of the sort." She was getting to her feet as she snapped the retort. "I'm not going to be any burden to you. I just mean I feel awful. How would you expect a poor greenhorn to feel after she has been beaten, dropped on her head, and forced to sleep on the ground in clothes that fit her like a haystack cover?"

He laughed, glad that she could joke about her own woes. "You'll live. Fumble around in there and get the rifle and cartridges. I'll get the ponies saddled."

He hurried away, feeling a little better for the exchange of pleasantries, even though he was acutely aware of the danger in this delay. He saddled up hastily but with due care, knowing how critical a loosened cinch might turn out to be. Then he led the broncs back to where the girl waited in the darkness.

"Try this bronc on for size," he invited. "I'll give you a hand up and we'll adjust the stirrups for you. Grab hold of the saddle horn and up you go."

He groped for her, guiding her in the pitch blackness and boosting her into the saddle. "It's the Diablo horse for you," he explained. "A smart animal and plenty gentle. Can you remember to cock a gun if I give you one?"

"You might try me."

He went into the hut, bringing out the ornate gun belt which had been part of Diablo's showy equipment. Reaching up he buckled it around her waist. "Not a very good fit, but it won't fall off unless you do. Where's the rifle?"

"In my hand."

"Let me have it. The saddle boot is on my bronc. We'll hope we won't need it, but it'll be just as well to have it along."

She handed over both weapon and cartridges, waiting silently while he attended to the multiple details of preparation. Finally he was satisfied. "All ready, I hope. Now you'll have to climb down again and lead the bronc until we're clear of the cedars."

She uttered a little groan of dismay. "Can't I ride?"

"Not unless you want to get knocked out of the saddle by a tree limb. What's wrong? Do you feel that bad?"

"No. It's — I can't — I simply mean that I'm afraid I can't keep these pants up!"

In spite of the tension of the moment Wayne had to laugh. Her woebegone voice was almost as funny as her predicament. "Hold 'em with one hand and lead the bronc with the other," he advised. "I'd be glad to help you only it's one of those things that a gent can't very well do for a lady."

"A lady, he says," she retorted. "When I was on my good behavior he called me nasty names. Now that I've run wild he calls me a lady! I'm glad it's dark."

"I'm starting," he broke in. "Try to stick close behind my horse. This is no time to get lost."

He worked his way into the thicket, purposely making slow progress and listening to make certain that she was staying close. Maybe he could have made it a little easier for her, but it didn't seem like a good time to baby her. There was a lot of rough travel ahead of them and she might as well get used to doing for herself.

16

They broke out into the open quickly enough and he boosted her back into the saddle, helping her to find the stirrups while she struggled to get the oversize attire into some semblance of a reasonable fit. Suddenly he knew that he was watching her movements, seeing them instead of merely sensing them in the darkness. He wheeled sharply, studying the sky in the east. In spite of the clouds it was graying there, lightening the blackness of the wooded hills.

"Morning," he said briefly, vaulting into his own saddle. "Worse than I thought. Let's make tracks fast."

He kept to the rock ledge for only a short distance, throwing caution to the winds as he struck out across country to the south. Leaving tracks didn't mean anything now. If they could reach Oro City it wouldn't be important. If they didn't make it, then it wouldn't be important either.

Their general direction was toward the southeast, the main idea being to keep within the hill country for several miles and then to break out into the easier going of the valley when concealment was no longer a factor. It might well have been smart strategy except that they ran squarely into three riders as they swung into the gulch which connected the old Wayne place with the trail to Tinaja. It was a meeting which gave neither party any warning. All Wayne knew was that he was just beginning to feel a little safer when suddenly there were those three horsemen looming out of the morning mists.

"Cut back!" he ordered swiftly. "Keep to the gulch and run!"

Almost at the same instant he heard a familiar voice yell, "Lookit, Monty. There's both of 'em. I told yuh there was two o' the polecats!"

One of the other men was less wordy but more active. A gun boomed resoundingly between the steep walls of the gulch, and Wayne heard the whine of a slug as it passed him. He leaned forward, yanking the rifle from its boot as he swung his bronc to follow Jan. He didn't suppose he would be any more accurate with it than he would have been with a six gun, but there was something awe-inspiring about a rifle. It might scare the enemy enough to gain time.

Two more bullets sped by him as he twisted his body and took hasty aim. The three riders were coming after him at full gallop now, their shooting betraying their haste as well as the motion of their horses. Wayne fired twice, then reached around to pull the bay to a sliding halt. Even as the animal broke stride the rifle was slamming again, its slugs aimed a little more steadily as the jolting motion ended.

There was a yell of dismay from the enemy and one of them toppled from the saddle, crashing to earth in a manner that was grimly satisfying to the marksman. Another shot halted pursuit entirely as the other two men took to the brush. Only then did Wayne urge the bay into renewed action.

He overtook Jan quickly. She had held the black to an easy pace, evidently unwilling to separate herself from Wayne.

"Keep going," he ordered. "We've got to run for it, so don't hang back when I tell you to hustle."

"What have I got a gun for?"

He shook his head. "Don't itch to be a heroine unless it's necessary. You won't look any prettier dead. Git!"

274

There was no sound of immediate pursuit as they dashed into the clearing which had once been home to Perry Wayne. Jan started to ask a question at sight of the shattered cabin, but he motioned to the south, interrupting her. "Another trail out that way. We'll try it and hope they haven't closed it off."

Almost as he spoke there came the sound of two shots from their immediate rear. They were answered by two others from some distance to the north and a single from out toward the valley.

"Signals," he guessed. "They're closing in."

She was holding to the saddle horn with one hand as they slammed into the turn which opened south. Wayne knew a real misgiving. The girl was not as good a rider as she might have been, certainly not expert enough for the wild chase which lay ahead of them.

The worry was forgotten, however, as another pair of gunshots sounded from the hill country ahead of them. "Pull up," he snapped. "No use trying this one. They've got us boxed."

"Can't we find a place to hide around the ranch back there? Any place where we can hold them off until some honest men appear. Then I'll show myself. Brack won't dare let them shoot me."

"Don't fool yourself," he retorted as he swung his mount and motioned toward the ranch house. "You heard what Jabe Conree shouted back there in the gulch. They spotted the black outfit and think you're Diablo. You can't let yourself be seen over gun sights any more than I can."

She let that sink in as they raced past the house. Wayne pointed with his rifle toward a break in the steep hills west of the clearing. "Back that way. It's our only chance now. We'll hold 'em off as long as we can and hope for a break."

She did not speak but hung on grimly, fighting for her seat on the black horse as they pelted headlong for the opening. Wayne cut the pace as soon as they were on the sheltered slope behind the ranch. It would take a little time for the Brack forces to organize, so he decided that it would be worth the risk to slow down and avoid having the girl take a spill.

"Take it easy," he advised. "They won't rush us here until they've got the proper men in the front ranks, trusted thugs who won't make the mistake of taking a prisoner."

They eased the horses to a walk as they

started to climb, presently slanting off on a sort of ledge which angled away to the northeast. Everywhere in front of them were the sheer cliffs which characterized that section of mountains — the sort of cliffs that sheltered the glen where they had passed the night. Jan surveyed the country dubiously but she made no complaint, simply riding a little closer to Wayne as though to express her fear that they might be entering a trap.

The angular ledge became a horizontal flaw in the rimrock and Wayne signaled a halt. "Now we lead the broncs," he said quietly. "Walk close to the cliff and don't look down. The pony will take care of himself if you just let him. It's not as narrow as it looks from here."

It was too narrow for comfort, but not for much of a distance. Wayne crossed the danger spot confidently, never looking back until he was on easier ground where a huge slash had been gouged out of the mountain's bald face. Then he merely gave the girl a nod of encouragement as she came toward him. Her face was pale, but she managed a smile as she said shakily, "A fine place to take a lady who has to hold up her pants while she walks!"

"You'll do, Jan," he approved. "It takes

nerve to joke when you're plumb scared. Now let's get the broncs back into this slot out of sight. We can hold that trail against any kind of force they throw against us. I just hope they don't think to put riflemen in any of the treetops though. They could get mighty annoying."

Almost as he spoke there was a shout from the distant valley, and he motioned quickly. "Get down flat and watch. I'll take the broncs. Don't show anything but keep your eyes on that break in the trees off there to the right." He pointed down to an open patch which showed lighter color in the tufted carpet of dark greens which stretched before them. From their position on the cliff they were looking out across the treetops, commanding the valley quite satisfactorily.

Jan glanced around at him as she took her post. "What about that trail behind us? Do I need my gun?"

He restrained a smile. She was talking guns as though the subject were an old familiar one. "No need. They won't find us that soon. Just keep your eyes on the valley. You can listen for any sounds on the ledge."

He took the horses down the slight incline which led to a deeper hole in the solid rock. The slant was in itself a safeguard against bullets from the lower valley, but he knew that slugs might ricochet from the stone overhang and endanger the ponies at the rear. Consequently he led both animals around a protecting bend in the crevice which extended into the mountain, tying them securely before returning to the girl. He had examined this giant flaw in the cliff many times before and knew exactly what it was worth as a defensive post. Actually the mountain side had been given a double split by some prehistoric earthquake, a huge chunk having fallen clear while the balance of the vertical strata between the two cracks had settled to form the ledge on which they were situated. The accumulated debris of ages had partly filled the narrowing crevice behind them and it was on this fill that the ponies were tethered. It was a position capable of being stoutly defended, and he hoped to hold it until such time as Brack's reasons for attack would be questioned by others in the attacking party. It seemed like the only real hope.

He ran back to throw himself on his belly beside Jan, so placed that he could see along the narrow back trail and still have a view of the valley below. "Anything?" he asked.

"Yes. A rider crossed the opening just as you came back. Moving from left to right."

"Trailing us. That's really not an opening

down there but only a part of the big clearing. The rest of it is hidden by the contours of the lower slope." He shifted a little as he spoke, pulling the rifle around so that it could cover the ledge. "Keep watching the gap. I'll cover this rim."

The sun was beginning to break through the scattered clouds above the distant mountains to the east, burning away the overcast which had come on during the night, when Jan uttered a little exclamation. "There he goes back again! The same man!"

Wayne looked quickly, just in time to see a rider disappearing behind the trees. "Going back in a hurry," he muttered. "That means he has spotted our tracks and knows we're somewhere up here on the cliff. So he goes back for help. I wonder why he didn't signal with gunshots like the other boys did?"

"I could guess."

He did not reply. There was no point in dwelling upon the grimmer aspects of the situation. All that counted now was to remain alert and hope for some sort of break which was not yet predictable.

They waited for a good twenty minutes, seeing nothing and hearing no sounds except a couple of distant shouts. Then a pair of gunshots boomed faintly from somewhere far to the south.

"Could that be help coming?" Jan asked.

"What help? So far as I know there isn't anyone anywhere who knows about us or wants to help. We're alone in our misery, like the Ishmaelite. Every man's hand raised against us."

"Sometimes you sound downright literary," she commented. "It makes me almost sorry that I never managed to learn more than the first two lines of 'Mary had a little lamb'."

"You'd do better to take a lesson in shooting. For one thing you might practice reloading that cannon you're holding so belligerently. The skill might come in handy, and it'll make you relax. This way you'll wear yourself out gripping it so tight."

"So I'm a fraud," she acknowledged, chuckling a little. "I tried to be flippant, and all the time you knew I was holding on for dear life."

"White knuckles betray a glib tongue," he said with mock solemnity. "That sounds like a good quote but I made it up out of my own head. Congratulate me."

"Now who's doing it? I'll bet you're scared, too — but don't admit it. Just tell me what to do with this gun."

He explained without looking around,

diverting his glance from the valley only when she asked questions. Before long she was loading and unloading the six gun with reasonable skill, and was quite proud of herself.

"Now take the rifle and pass me the hawg-leg," he directed. "You can keep the guns loaded and I'll shoot 'em. Real Kentucky blockhouse tactics."

The exercise provided occupation for the better part of an hour, during which time there was neither sight nor sound of the enemy. Meanwhile the sun was mounting, bringing a warmth which Wayne knew would soon become uncomfortable.

The waiting became tedious, and it was clear that Jan was losing some of her careful poise. More to take her mind away from the danger than for any other reason Wayne remarked, "By the way, I don't suppose you knew that you were helping to defend a gold mine, did you?"

"A what?"

"A gold mine, in a small way. There's gold in the hole where I left the broncs. I suppose the flaw in the cliff contained a vein of the stuff, enough to weaken the mountain and let it separate at that point when the old upheaval came along. That's where the gold came from that they found at my house and used to prove your uncle's murder on me."

"That part was never entirely clear to me, you know," she reminded him. "Maybe you'd better straighten me out on that part of it."

He explained everything, much as he had done for Pegleg Clancy. She heard him through in silence, then remarked thoughtfully, "You're one up on me. Brack beat me out of a mine, but he swindled you out of a mine and a ranch."

"And my liberty. That was the big item. The gold mine isn't much, I'm afraid. I don't think there are any really big gold deposits in these mountains. They've prospected the Javelinas threadbare since your uncle made his strike, but they have never found anything except small pot holes of the stuff. I figure it's the same way on this side of the basin. I hoped to take enough out of here to clear my land and set me up in the cattle business. No more. That was why I kept it so quiet. A gold rush can ruin a country too fast to suit me, so I kept my mouth shut because I didn't want the hills overrun by a horde of gold-mad prospectors."

He broke off as more shots sounded from the distance. They listened intently but could not guess at the meaning. Certainly there was no sign of anyone moving in the valley below them, but Wayne did not believe that the hunt had missed them. That rider Jan had seen was evidence to the contrary.

They killed time with talk until by mid-afternoon each knew the other's story in rather complete detail. It had been hot up there on the ledge but mutual interest helped them to forget it, the only real discomfort being the shortage of water. Wayne insisted upon conserving the tiny supply in the canteens, remembering that they might be in for quite a siege.

"It's worse for the broncs," he told her. "We'll make out for a day or so, but they'll have to suffer. The best I can do for them is to keep them back out of the sun."

The purple shadows had drifted well across the valley when the first break came in the long, dreary wait. Two riders appeared briefly in an opening a little to the left of the one they had been watching so closely — two riders with a pack horse trailing behind them. There was just a fraction of a second to see that the pack animal carried a bulky burden.

"They're back," Jan breathed. "Now what?"

"I wish I knew. More than that I wish we had opened fire on that other rider. It was our big mistake when we sat tight."

"Why was it?"

"We recognized the strategy, but we didn't have sense enough to make a countermove. Brack's men spotted us but made no move against us because they wanted to lead the rest of the hunt to some other spot. We should have made noise enough to spoil their game for them. Now they're back, free to wipe us out without witnesses."

"Would it be any good to fire a few shots now?"

"I doubt it. We'd just disclose our true position."

He stood up, trying to catch sight of the riders who had moved down there beneath the trees. A rifle bullet whined over his head with great promptness, smashing into fragments against the rock wall of the niche.

"I guess that's an answer to both points," he muttered, dropping flat once more. "They already know where we are and they're not afraid to make some noise about it." He was studying the trees as he spoke. Suddenly he rolled slightly and thrust the rifle barrel out over the edge of the precipice. Sighting carefully, he fired, then followed with a pair of shots as fast as he could work the lever of the rifle.

"Sniper in a tree out there, maybe three or four hundred yards."

"Did you hit him?"

"Not likely at that range. All I could sight on was a little patch of smoke. It ought to cool his ardor, though, and if noise will help it's a bid for attention."

"Do you think it will do any good?"

"No."

There was a dead silence between them until Wayne muttered ruefully, "Anyway, it helps me make up my mind about that little scouting trip I was considering. I'd be a sitting duck if I ventured out on the ledge now."

Presently he pulled off his hat and poked it out over the brink on the end of the rifle barrel. It was an ancient dodge but it brought quick results. Two shots boomed almost in unison, the slugs glancing from rocks high overhead.

"They're closing in below," he commented. "Although I don't see why. We're sheltered from any fire from that point, and there's no way to scale the cliff."

"Maybe they're trying to keep us pinned down while someone else comes up along the ledge."

"I hope you're right. I'd sure like the

chance to work on Brack and his boys if they come at us from that angle."

"Then you don't think that's the idea?"

"Not with Brack running the show. He doesn't make any moves except smart ones. We've got to look out for that kind."

Twice more as the warm dusk fell across the valley Wayne drew fire by shoving his hat into view. "We'll let them do the noise-making for us," he said quietly. "Just in case there might be somebody around to hear. They've got more ammunition to waste than we have."

"And it's Brack who's supposed to be the smart one," Jan murmured.

He tossed her a quick grin. "Us fellers up here ain't so danged stupid neither," he chuckled, putting the drawl on thickly again. "I even got a hunch on what they're plannin', and I'm hopin' it won't work."

Night came on rapidly then, and Wayne turned the rifle over to Jan. "Time to post our night guard," he whispered. "Keep down and stay quiet. I won't be long."

"What are you going to do?" There was a trace of panic in the query.

"Nothing desperate. I just want to make sure we're not surprised during the night." He disappeared into the darkness along the ledge, working his way to the point where the treacherous path was narrowest. He worked there for several minutes, then returned to the niche.

"A few loose cobbles and some empty cartridge cases in strategic spots," he explained. "Anybody coming along there in the dark is certain to dislodge something. We'll hear a clink or two even if he doesn't slide over the edge, which is almost too much to hope for."

The temperature dropped sharply with the coming of night, and presently Wayne realized that he was shivering. Jan had not complained, but he knew that she must be even colder. Those black garments of El Diablo were not made for cold weather.

"Stay down and keep watch," he cautioned. "I'm going to steal the saddle blankets from our poor neglected steeds. That Diablita Hermosa outfit can't be very warm."

"It isn't," she agreed, teeth chattering as she tried to speak.

He returned quickly with the blankets, dropping one across the girl's shoulders as he resumed his position at her side. "Better to smell horsy than to freeze. Anything sound off while I was gone?"

"Something like footsteps, I thought. It was — Oh-oh! There it is again. Listen!"

After a brief flurry of sound there was complete silence once more, and presently Jan asked, "What did that name mean that you called me a few minutes ago? I know enough Spanish to translate Diablo Negro into Black Devil, but after that I'm stuck."

"Just a slight alteration. Diablita would be a little devil, female variety."

"Scarcely complimentary. Was the other word as bad?"

"Hermosa? I suppose you know exactly what it means and you're just fishing for a compliment. But I'll tell you. It means pretty."

"Oh," she said, her tone carrying a note of confusion which was in marked contrast to her usual self-sufficiency. Compliments seemed to bother her more than danger.

Wayne smiled to himself in the darkness.

There was another of those long, silent waits, broken finally by a sound of movement from far below. Wayne inched forward until he could look down into the black emptiness in front of him. No flicker of movement could be seen, but there was a distinct rustle of movement now, even an occasional rattle of loose rock as groping feet blundered in the night.

He reached out to pick up a couple of loose cobbles that were handy, pitching them out over the sheer drop. There was a surprisingly long silence before he could hear the clatter of the stones bouncing from the lower edge of the rocky cliff. With the thud of further descent came a shout of anger and then a yelp of pain.

"Get on with it!" a voice shouted. "Don't whine about pebbles. Get moving!"

"More rocks," Wayne snapped excitedly. "I don't know what they're doing, but if rocks will bother 'em we'll give 'em everything movable. That was Brack's voice."

Jan sprang up to help, but he uttered a quick word of warning. "Not too frisky. You'll go over the edge. Roll your rocks to the edge and shove 'em."

They cleaned off the nearby ledge quickly enough, setting up a disturbance below that was quite satisfying to hear. After the nerve-frazzling wait, it was good to be doing something — especially something that was clearly annoying to the enemy.

Then Wayne changed the orders. "Roll 'em to the edge, but don't let 'em go," he whispered. "The boys have ducked so we'll wait till they come back. Might as well get some results for our work."

"What do you think they're trying to do?" she panted.

"I'd guess it's a blasting job. That pack horse we saw this afternoon was carrying what looked like a couple of kegs of blasting powder under a tarpaulin. It would be just like Smarty Brack to have spotted the nature of this flaw in the cliff and to figure that a good blast would dislodge the big wedge of stone that we're on."

"Do you think he's right?" The question was only a little anxious, a tribute to the girl's self-control.

"I hope not."

"Would it be safer to move out on that solid ledge?"

"I reckon I'd rather take my chances here. That ledge might crumple before this hunk of rock would slip. It's not a nice spot, one way or another, but I'll gamble on this wedge. A good heavy charge of explosive, well drilled into the base, might do the trick, but we're not going to let Brack have any chance for drilling. I'm guessing he won't get us with any surface charge."

She seemed to be considering the point. After a minute or two she inquired solemnly, "Did you ever go 'coon hunting?"

"What? Oh, you mean we're treed like a 'coon and we're just waiting to see whether the hunter can shake us down."

"Exactly. Kind of a queer feeling, isn't it?"

"Don't think about it. Just shove up a few more rocks and then try to get some rest. It'll be a long night."

An hour passed before they heard anything more from below. Then it was only the faint scrape of a boot heel some distance out from the cliff base. Evidently Brack's men were biding their time, waiting for something to happen before going on with their mining operations.

"I'll get ready," Wayne whispered. "It looks

to me like the blasting crew is waiting for some sort of covering attack, so I'm guessing that it means a gunhawk up here."

"Any orders for me, General?" Jan asked quietly.

"Yes. Stay right here and be ready to shove rocks. I'll take the right flank and cover the ledge." He laid down his rifle long enough to shove a couple of boulders into position in front of him, then he raised the weapon again, holding it so that he might swing it in either direction. Then the waiting continued.

It was a weary wait, but finally his alert ear caught a stealthy sound from along the cliff face. "Get ready, and keep down," he called softly over his shoulder. "Over with the rocks when you hear them moving around down below."

They waited breathlessly until a low whistle shrilled from somewhere very close at hand. Wayne was staring into the blackness of the night, but he could scarcely make out the bulge of the cliff. The man out there was still only a sound in the darkness. Then the signal was answered from below and at once there was the sound of movement from the valley. The blasting crew was returning to the attack, depending on some sort of covering fire from above.

Bedlam broke loose in three places. Jan's boulders began to pelt the lower fringe of the cliff while two guns began to yammer at each other along the ledge. Wayne fired first at the sound of rolling pebbles, but then both men were firing at the enemy's gun flashes. It lasted only a matter of seconds and then the mountains were silent except for the tiny clatter of displaced pebbles trickling down across the cliff's face.

"Are you all right?" Jan breathed.

"Sure. You?"

"Fine. But some of those bullets sounded mighty close."

"One of 'em was too close. It spattered hot lead on my left hand." He licked away a trickle of blood as he spoke, but clenched his fingers a couple of times, determining that no real damage had been suffered.

"What happened to the other man?"

"I couldn't tell. Sounded like two of 'em, and I think I must have scored at least one hit. Anyway he's ducked out."

They fell silent as other voices sounded from below. The words were indistinguishable at first, but the tone was clear. Wayne could almost be positive in his identification of Brack. The man was urging his followers on, and they were not at all keen about running into any more rocks.

Presently there came a bold hail from the dark depths. Brack was throwing secrecy to the winds. "Hey, Rory! Truesdale! What's happened? Give us some help, damn you!"

There was no answer, and Wayne grunted in satisfaction. "Finnegan and Truesdale, eh? I hope I plugged Finnegan."

"I don't hear any answer from either of them," Jan said, her voice dry even in her excitement. "What happens now?"

They didn't wait long to learn. The low-toned argument in the forest seemed to subside, and they could hear stealthy movements centering on a spot which was no longer directly below the listeners. Once Wayne tossed a small rock in the direction of the busy sounds, but there was no reaction. Only that shuffle of feet as men moved back and forth between the woods and the cliff.

"Seems like they've decided to burn their powder over there to one side," he murmured. "Our cobbles won't reach them there, and a good blast stands a chance of succeeding. After all, it would be concussion that would topple this slab if it goes."

"You don't sound so confident now."

"But I am. I still don't think anything short of a deep, well-drilled job will get results."

"Which we keep them from doing."

"And which they won't have time to do. Remember there's a time limit on their neat little scheme. Somebody is almost certain to ride back into the valley come morning, and they can't afford any raw stuff then."

"Who, for instance?"

"Any of that posse. And then there was a stranger in Tinaja who was getting a little aggravated at Brack. I let him know that Brack was playing him for a sucker, and I'm almost ready to hope that he might take a hand."

"How would that help us?"

"Because he's a pretty important jigger, I think. If Clinton Moss brings in lawmen there will be other friends of mine in Tinaja to steer them out in this direction."

"Clinton Moss?" she repeated in astonishment.

"That's right. I guess I forgot to tell you about him. His daughter was asking about you, only I didn't know for sure who you were or why you were at Brack's, so I kept quiet."

"Don't tell me Vicky Moss is in Tinaja!"

"She was a couple of days ago." He chuckled suddenly, realizing what Jan must be thinking. "Sorry I couldn't put in a good word for you. Both Moss and his daughter

296

seemed to be mighty certain that you'd gotten yourself into some kind of a mess. They didn't even suspect how big a mess it was."

"They'll imagine plenty!" She seemed more disgusted than worried. "Only they won't consider danger like this to be the worst part of it. All they'll think about is the fact that I've been out in the hills alone with a strange man for a couple of days and nights."

He couldn't think of anything to say to that, but noise from below relieved him of the need for further talk. The tempo of action down there speeded up suddenly, men running back and forth without attempting to hide the sound of their actions. Wayne decided that they were digging, evidently planting the blasting powder in the loose shale at the base of the cliff. He inched forward, shoving the rifle out of the edge of the rock. Shooting would not be a very accurate proposition in the darkness, but he thought he could make somebody rather uncomfortable down there if there should come a decent chance.

Presently the noise of hasty movement died away, and he could hear only the quick breathing of the girl beside him. Then, some distance out from the precipice, a man's voice growled an order, and Wayne tucked

297

his rifle into position, trying to estimate the position of its sights.

He was ready when a match flared below him, and just for an instant he caught the silhouette of gun sights against the glare, a silhouette which blended into the dark shadow of the man who was trying to shield the match with his body. In that instant Wayne squeezed the trigger and the shadow pitched forward, extinguishing the light in falling.

"Lucky shot," he commented with dry satisfaction as he slid backward to escape the angry hail of lead which must have been aimed at his gun flash. "This rifle handles fine. Nice of Brack to buy guns that fit me so well."

The firing ended as quickly as it had begun, and he pushed into position again. Men were talking again, louder this time as anger made them careless. It was quite clear that Brack was trying to drive another member of his crew to the chore of lighting the fuse, and nobody wanted to take the risk.

"Light it yourself," a voice snarled. "I ain't lookin' fer none o' what Dimmick got. I kin fight but I ain't —"

"Look, Chan," another voice cut in. "We might —" The talk dropped a notch, and

Wayne could not make out any more of the words. He thought, however, that the latest suggestion was being carried out, for after a bit of low-voiced talk there came another sound of activity. Cradling his rifle carefully he aimed downward as before but no light came to guide him. Men were moving around down there, but they were working in complete darkness. Finally the sounds of movement ceased, only a rustle of footsteps sounding from back among the trees.

Then a second match flashed into life, this time partly concealed by foliage. It was not where Wayne had expected it, and by the time he could swing his rifle there was an added flare of light. The match was being applied to loose powder on the ground.

Apparently the enemy had laid an open train of powder from the fuse to a sheltered spot, but they had misjudged the thickness of the trees over their heads. Wayne could still see the figure of the man who had held the match, and he snapped a quick shot as the fellow started to run away. Again it was a lucky shot but he did not wait to see more than the fall of his second victim.

"Get back!" he ordered briskly, grabbing Jan's arm. "This time we get it."

"Is it safer back here?" Jan asked a little breathlessly as he hustled her into the opening where the horses stamped nervously. "I don't like this rock hanging over our heads."

"Protection," he assured her, hoping his guess was right. "Rather that than loose stuff falling on us."

He stopped to listen as they rounded the corner of rock. A man was yelling for help, evidently the man who had been shot down after lighting the powder train. He was cursing his companions, his curses mounting in pitch and ferocity as the powder burned closer to the cliff.

"Come back, damn you!" the voice shrieked. "Don't leave me here, you dirty cowards." There was a lot more of it, but Wayne scarcely heard the words. The important thing was that he was listening to the harsh tones of Chandler Brack. The harshness had turned to a whine now, but there could be no question about the identity. Brack was lying helpless beside the scene of an imminent explosion, deserted by his own men.

The bitter irony in it brought a sense of fierce, grim satisfaction to Wayne, but he did not forget his own danger. Pulling the girl toward him, he ordered briskly, "Lie down. Less chance of getting knocked down when the bang comes."

She huddled against him as they flattened

themselves on the rock floor. He could feel her tremble as he put his arm around her. Out there in the night Brack's fear-crazed voice still cursed the deserters, but Wayne forced his thoughts away from his partial triumph. "Sorry I had to meet you at a time like this, Jan. If anything happens I want you to know I'm mighty sorry about what I said that first day. You're a good scout."

She twisted in his grasp and kissed him firmly. It was then that the mountain shuddered under the force of a booming blast which seemed to pick them up bodily and slam them down against the rock. For some moments they were both too stunned to move, but then Wayne knew that the worst of the danger was over. The powder had done its worst, but the big wedge of rock was still firmly imbedded in the split cliff. Maybe it had shifted a few inches one way or another but it was still solid.

He did not move until the sound of falling debris ceased. Then he murmured softly into the girl's ear. "Do your kisses always have as rough an effect as that?"

It seemed to require an effort for her to bring her mind to the question, but then she giggled a little. There was a shade of hysteria in the sound, but she controlled it and made her voice as steady as ever as she retorted, "Would you figure it too great a risk in the future?"

He settled that point promptly enough. Then he stood up, lifting her to her feet and keeping an arm around her. "We'd better take a peek at things," he proposed. "Smells like something burning down below."

They crawled quickly to the rim, cautious lest some of the outer rock might have been loosened by the explosion. It all seemed solid enough, however, and the sight that met their eyes was almost worth the risk. The loosely buried blasting powder had spent its main force in uprooting shale and small stones, throwing them as projectiles among the nearer trees. At the same time the blast had set fires which were now illuminating the broken, shattered pines.

"I imagine that's what hell must look like," Wayne said slowly. "Fire and destruction for a hundred feet in every direction."

He could see the twisted body of a man lying near a burning bush and he studied it for a moment as the flames brought it clearly into view. "It's Brack, all right," he pronounced. "The blast finished what my bullet started. Naturally, I don't feel a bit sorry but I'm wondering how it'll work out. I'll never be able to force a confession out of him now."

"You never would have," Jan said tersely. "And you're better off with him out of the way. There ought to be a weak spot in some of his gang now that he can't force them into line. I'd think that man Conree was a good bet."

"He was," Wayne replied, still inclined to cut his words off pessimistically. "But I think he's the jasper I plugged in that first skirmish."

He stood up suddenly, his tone changing. "Time for that later. Now We've got to get out of here. That fire's getting hotter."

"But it can't reach us, can it?"

"Not in any volume; the cliff's too bare. But it can make this pocket mighty hot with the wind sucking the flames up toward us."

Even as he spoke he got a nose full of smoke. The brush along the lower face of the cliff was beginning to blaze and it seemed clear that the whirling currents of air along the mountain were beating the fire back upwind into the main valley. It meant that a very hot fire was going to be burning directly below the position of the refugees.

"Might as well be in a chimney," Wayne choked. "Get hold of the black horse. We'll get out while we can still make it."

She was close behind him as he untied both horses, handing her the black's reins.

"You mean along that little ledge in the darkness?"

"It won't be so light again until morning. The blaze will light it and the smoke hasn't begun to hang yet. Hold tight to the bronc; ponies sometimes get crazy in fire."

"But it's so awfully narrow."

"We came over it once. Leave the saddle; we don't have time for anything like that. Come along." He couldn't let her weaken now. She had to handle her own share of the getaway chore if he could possibly badger her into it. "Keep close to my bronc," he snapped. "Hug the inside wall, but don't overdo it. The black will take care of himself if you don't do anything foolish. Snappy now!"

Both horses shied wildly as they were led out to the rim. The fire below them was beginning to fan out in broader bands of flame as it spread both ways along the foot of the cliff. Wayne spoke soothingly but firmly, getting the bay under control with a stern hand and trying to reach the black horse with his voice. He could hear Jan trying to imitate his tone, but there was no time for delay. Already tongues of flame were beginning to sweep up past them, the acrid smoke of pine forming a choking pall around the ledge. There would be no time

304

for two trips; Jan had to take care of herself and a horse if they were all to get out alive.

"Short grip on the reins," he called back to her. "Don't let him start tossing his head. Come on."

He fought to keep his eyes clear, knowing that the danger point was directly ahead. If the blast had not loosened any of the narrow section of ledge they would probably get out all right. Even with the thought something rolled under his foot and he felt himself slipping. There was an instant thought of the ledge cracking away from the cliff, but then he knew that he had simply stepped into his own booby trap. Loose stones and an empty shell case had rolled under his tread.

It was almost fatal at that. He had to catch himself on all fours, releasing the bay's bridle as he fell, but luckily there was solid rock under his fingers when he went down. Behind him he could hear Jan's gasp of dismay, but it ended in another sort of exclamation so he didn't pause to reassure her. Instead he stayed on his knees until he had swept the narrow place clear with fingers that still trembled. Then he felt something sticky, something which looked brown on his hands in the weird glow of the fire.

"Hold it just a minute," he yelled above the increasing roar of the flames. "I'll round the turn and come back for you."

He led the bay quickly across the dangerous spot and past the projecting bulge of the cliff. They were scarcely on the wider ledge when he found what he was expecting — the dark bulk of a man's body on the rock. It was no time for mawkish sentiment so he reached down to grab the still form by one arm, heaving quickly as revulsion swept over him. "I hope it was Finnegan," he grunted to himself as the dark form plunged over the side. "Anyway the trail had to be cleared."

He left the bay and went back to take the girl's arm. "All clear now. Keep your face to the cliff and the smoke won't catch you quite so badly."

"Was there — ?" she faltered.

"Never mind. Keep your mind on getting out." He shoved her along ahead of him, steering her across the narrow part as he kept the black horse under control with his other hand. It was getting hotter every second, but it did not take long for them to reach the safer trail beyond.

"Catch on," he said, passing the reins back to her. "I'll lead again. Stick with my bronc." He knew that she was getting shaky so he made himself sound as stern as possible, trying to keep her busy enough so that she wouldn't crack.

In another minute they were clear of the smoke but he kept going for a full hundred yards, by that time reaching the gentler slope which led into the valley. Then he pulled up with a cheerful, "Clean away. Can you ride a bit now?"

There was no answer. Indistinctly against the now distant fire he could see the girl's form suddenly go limp, dragging the black's head down as she slumped to the ground.

"Steady again, Cottonfoot," he ordered. "It's happened."

He hurried back to drop on one knee beside her, blaming himself for the way he had kept driving her, even though he knew it had been necessary. Her face seemed clammy to his touch and her pulse rate was slow but there did not seem to be anything seriously wrong. Just a good faint, he decided, unfastening the black's reins from her wrist. Reaction after having kept up on nerve for so long. He lifted her gently and carried her ahead far enough to get clear of the restless ponies, then he laid her down where a little patch of grass edged the trail. After that he went back to get the horses, running a rope between them. "Take it easy, fellers," he murmured. "We got a new kind of trouble for a minute or two."

18

She was stirring a little when he knelt beside her once more. He put an arm behind her head, holding her gently as he whispered, "Take it easy. We've got all night, or what little is left of it."

"What happened? Did I — ?"

"You did. One of the best-timed faints a lady ever pulled. And you were entitled to it. Now lie quiet a bit longer and you'll be as good as new."

"I'm a sissy," she half whispered. "Let me get up and we'll be on our way."

"You're a real salty character, partner," he corrected. "And you get five minutes to catch your breath. I don't think we have to be in any great rush now."

She moved her head contentedly against the curve of his arm. "Then we're out of danger?"

"Mostly."

"Then maybe I'll rest a minute or so. I —

I rather like it this way."

He let his arm tighten a little. "I'm not feeling any real pain myself."

They both laughed then, a shade of nervous hysteria in the merriment, but still good laughter. It occurred to Wayne that there had been a remarkable lot of laughing taking place in the past few hours, considering the nature of the events which had been taking place. It was a bit peculiar that a man should want to laugh — but he knew that he did.

Brief minutes later a rattle of shots in the distance recalled him to the stern realities of the case. Not only was there still a real peril from Brack's beaten but probably vindictive followers, but there was the serious danger from the fire. The light southeasterly breeze was keeping the conflagration pinned pretty well to the cliff, but there was a certain amount of spreading taking place and daylight might bring a shift of wind that could turn the whole valley into a vast fire pit.

"Let's go, Jan," he said, pulling her up. "We'd better get out of here while we can still make it."

"What do you suppose that shooting meant?"

"Hard to tell, but we can hope that it was

310

Brack's boys getting fouled up with some honest citizens."

He boosted her to the back of the black bronc. "Grab him around the neck if you need to," he suggested. "I won't get jealous. We'll take it easy and you'll find that bareback riding isn't so awfully hard."

They went slowly down the trail into the clearing behind the ruined ranch house, a general lightening of the gloom warning that daylight was fast approaching. Wayne had been considering the chances of a dash for the open valley in the event of a spreading of the fire, but he decided that it would be too much of a gamble. The girl could never stay on a horse for any such ride. Better to stick to this clearing.

"We'll try the house," he told her. "Unless the fire gets mighty bad we'll be safer there than anywhere else."

They left the horses tied to the weathered rail by the back door. It put the animals in a spot where they might be exposed to possible gunfire, but there was no choice in the matter. No better place was available and Wayne could only hope that the shooting was over.

As though to discourage the hope a shot rang out from a short distance to the east, followed by several others in rapid succession.

"Ought to be somebody on our side," he commented hopefully. "I hope they're winning."

Daylight was now distinct from the fire's glare but it was still too dark to see anything in the woodland. They waited in silence, remaining in the open until an exchange of shouts came to their ears.

"Take cover," Wayne directed. "We want to know what's going on before we show ourselves."

"But won't the horses give us away?"

"Maybe it's just as well. We can't tell friends from foes, but the other fellows will know when they see the broncs. They can announce themselves one way or another."

More shouting came to them then but it quickly became clear that no one was coming toward the cabin. Men were converging on the fire and beginning to fight it.

"That's good," Wayne commented. "Brack's outfit wouldn't be hanging around to fight fire. But we'll still sit tight. I've taken all the risks I want in the past few days."

Daylight came on quickly and he could see that the fire was dwindling, evidently well beaten down by the men whose voices could still be heard from time to time. Fortunately the light breeze had held, making the fire fighting easier. It seemed like a good sign to the anxious pair in the cabin, but both of them knew better than to let their hopes mount too high. There was still a serious chance that those men in the forest would shoot first and ask questions later.

In some ways the new uncertainty was worse than the tension of the night. Then they had known what confronted them; now they had to face the maddening realization that they were very close to an escape which they might never make good.

They talked it over in low tones, both of them entirely serious now, none of the flippancy creeping into the conversation. Banter had helped to keep spirits up during the night, but they were in no mood for it any longer. An hour passed, then another. By that time the fire seemed to be completely extinguished but still there was no sign of life in the adjacent woodland.

Then a queer, cracked voice came from the cover of the near trees. "Hey there! Are yuh in the house, Perry?"

"Clancy?"

"Yep. Don't git itchy with no shootin' iron, I'm comin' in."

"Come ahead."

The little man stumped into the clearing, followed by a broad-shouldered fellow in smoke-blackened range garb. Wayne suddenly recalled his doubts about Pegleg.

"Hold it, Clancy! Who's your friend?"

Pegleg stepped squarely in front of the other man but not before Wayne had spotted the bandage on the stranger's left forearm. "Don't git proddy, Perry," the little man shouted. "This here's a United States marshal, and that hole in his arm was drilled by a Brack slug. He ain't aimin' to do yuh no harm."

"Come on then but don't make any funny moves."

The pair approached slowly, halting about fifty feet from the shuttered window where Wayne had posted himself. It was the big man who did the talking then. "Take it easy, Wayne," he advised. "I know how you feel about this business, but you don't need to worry any longer. We've found out a lot in the past twenty-four hours. All we want to know is what happened to that girl who was at Brack's place."

"I'm right here." Jan spoke for herself. "I've been in very good hands."

"Good. I think your story will clean up everything for us. Look, Wayne, here's my badge. Maybe it will help you to believe me when I tell you that Mr. Clinton Moss stirred up a mighty loud stink with the territorial government until they sent me after you. Moss is even back there with some of the men who came along to help."

"That's shore right," Clancy affirmed. "We're tryin' to help, and Marshal Phillips is all fer yuh."

Other men were edging into the clearing now, and Wayne could see the familiar figures of Al Hulett and Ben Arms in the group. "I'm happy to be convinced," he announced. "Come around to the back door."

He turned to grin happily at Jan, really seeing her for the first time in daylight since the previous day. "Holy mackerel!" he exclaimed. "Are you the cute little blonde gal I saw the other day?"

She tried to match his grin, the effort quirking up the corners of a mouth that was just a ragged slit in a black face. Tears caused by smoke had washed little furrows in the soot until she made Wayne think of an Indian who had tried to put on his war paint while he was drunk. The yellow hair was full of pine needles and bits of ash, while the black garments of El Diablo hung in fantastic droops which made her look like nothing human.

"You're no bargain yourself," she retorted,

turning away with something almost like a sob.

There was no time for him to make peace. Clancy and Phillips were already at the door, both of them staring in amazement at the disreputable pair in front of them. Other men were close behind, and in a matter of minutes there was quite a gathering just outside the door of the ranch house. Everyone was trying to talk at the same time and in spite of the excitement Wayne gained several bits of information. The Brack strategy of the previous morning had been entirely successful in diverting the honest members of the posse from the real scene of action, but the whole scheme had been apparent to them by mid-afternoon.

It was Jabe Conree who had spilled the beans first. The man had been hard hit in that first skirmish in the gulch and had become delirious while being taken back to Tinaja. By the time they reached town his escort knew many things and suspected a lot more.

Then they found Marshal Phillips on the job. He had come in from Oro City with three deputies, and his actions were prompt when he heard the story. A new posse was organized but it was too late to do anything except to prepare for a ride into the foothills at dawn of the following day. Additional reports during the night made them fairly sure of the situation and they were quite prepared for what happened when they encountered the fleeing remnants of the Brack crowd next morning. There had been some fighting in which a couple of lawmen, including Phillips, had been wounded while three Brack gunmen had been put out of action. One of those was Boone Sabbath, and he had done a bit of talking before he died, telling in his own cold, fatalistic fashion the truth of the whole situation.

That much was clear to Wayne when he noticed the way Jan had slumped to the ground. Everyone had settled down to rest and to talk and everyone was more or less smoke stained, but the girl was a very picture of weariness and dismay.

"We'd better get out of here," he said abruptly. "One of you men let Miss Knight have your horse. Then you can start for Circle D while I go pick up the saddles we had to leave."

Clancy caught Wayne's eye, winking with something like sternness. "I'm with yuh, Perry. She can take my nag." He refused to listen to any counter proposals and they settled it that way, Marshal Phillips taking charge while Wayne and Clancy mounted the unsaddled broncs to head up the mountain.

As soon as they were out of earshot of the others Wayne threw a quizzical glance at his companion. "And why did you want to see me alone, my friend?" he inquired.

"How did yuh know I did?"

"You're about as subtle as a forty-five slug, Clancy. Go ahead. Get it out of your system."

The little man chuckled uneasily. "It's kinda like this. I wanted to tell yuh more about the Moss angle before yuh had a chance to see Moss. Me and Al Hulett kinda promoted it, but it plumb ran away with us. We figgered yuh was in a mighty bad jam when Brack told folks about yer two disguises so we took a chance on Moss bein' able to help."

There was much Wayne wanted to ask about but he didn't want to let Clancy ramble on. He simply asked, "Why Moss?"

"I'm tryin' to tell yuh, dammit! Al and me figgered yuh had to git help and nobody around Tinaja was willin' to buck Chan Brack. Clinton Moss was sore at him, though, particklerly when we told him about how the Three Toes had been salted fer suckers. He swore he'd shore learn Brack a lesson, so we told him some more."

318

"More what?"

"Jest about everything we knowed or could guess about Perry Wayne. How yuh got framed fer Lloyd's killin', how yuh got skun outa yer ranch, how yuh risked yer neck to tell Moss that the Three Toes was a washout. That was when the gal got into it."

"What gal? How did she get into it? Don't talk in so many riddles!"

"Moss' daughter. I reckon she was all lathered up over the way yuh stepped in and punched Finnegan fer her. Then she fair bubbled over when we spun her the rest o' the yarn. She claimed it was the most romantical thing she ever heard of, and she went right aboard of her pop to make him start pullin' wires fer help. The way she talked was fair sickenin', I'm tellin' yuh. She made out yuh was shore the white-haired boy, and before she got started with Moss toward Oro City I was beginnin' to be sorry I ever knowed sech a sweet-scented do-gooder as she was makin' yuh out to be. Anyway, that's how come I wanted to tell yuh about it."

Wayne stared at him in irritated perplexity. "It's a wonderful knack you have, Clancy, to miss all the important items and garble everything else. I gather that Moss was the one who brought in the law just in time for some of Brack's men to get scared and talk, but what in thunder does this Moss girl have to do with it that you seem so spooked up?"

Clancy spat disgustedly. "Hell's fire! Don't yuh see she's in love with yuh — anyway with the dam' romantical critter we made yuh out to be! And yuh got her to thank fer the way she put spurs to the old man and made him git the marshal on the job. Likewise she was all in a lather when nobody knowed fer sure what had happened with the other gal and yuhrself. I'm bettin' her pappy don't like it none, but she's shore got a bad case on yuh."

"You're loco, Clancy. Vicara Moss is flighty, I'll grant you, but she's not that silly."

"Wanta bet?"

He was still talking about it when they rode back into the clearing with both horses properly saddled. To the surprise of both men there were only two persons in sight. One was Al Hulett and the other was a trim little man in meticulous garments which looked completely out of place there.

It was Moss who explained after a brief word of congratulation to Wayne. "Marshal Phillips thought it would be better if I waited for you. We arrived just as the others were leaving."

Hulett threw in a word of explanation. "The marshal had to split his crews. Some of 'em are pickin' up bodies while a couple of men go with the ladies to get Miss Knight's duffle at Circle D."

"Which leaves us free for a few words which I'd like to have with you, Wayne," Moss said smoothly. "We can talk as we ride."

There was plenty of activity at Circle D. The federal men had set up headquarters there and were gathering together the loose threads of the case. Several corpses lay along the corral, including the blackened remains of Brack and Dimmick. So far as could be determined there had been a clean sweep of the whole Brack gang. All of the leaders were dead, while any surviving hired guns were making fast tracks out of the basin.

Wayne lingered to talk briefly with Marshal Phillips, then he went into the house. It was Vicara Moss who came to greet him, her eyes alight with something beyond the excitement which filled her voice. He met the swift flow of words with a short expression of thanks, then said firmly, "I'd like to talk to Jan, if I may. Alone."

The dark-haired girl faltered. "I — I'm afraid she isn't presentable. She —"

Wayne stepped past her, knocking on the door of the room Jan had occupied. "Jan. I want to talk to you."

"But I'm not dressed."

"Then get something on. I'm coming in."

He delayed only long enough to know that Vicky Moss was closing in behind him, then he opened the door and stepped into the room. He heard a little gasp of surprise from Jan and a murmur of annoyance from Vicky, then he closed the door, standing with his back to the rest of the room.

"Sorry," he half whispered. "But I had to get away."

"You may turn around," Jan told him, amused but still a little annoyed. "I'm dressed."

He swung to face her, seeing that she had changed to the tweed riding outfit, evidently ready for the trip to Tinaja. Soap and water had done wonders for her, but she was having something of a struggle with her hair.

"Primping, eh?" he commented. "I might have known it."

"And why shouldn't I? You certainly made it very clear that I needed it."

He pulled a long face. "Me and my big mouth. Got time to talk business for a couple of minutes?"

"Business?" She seemed faintly disappointed as well as puzzled.

"That's the way Moss made it sound. He has been selling me an idea ever since we left the cabin. Two ideas, rather."

"Yes?"

"In the first place he's all spooked up because his fair daughter has got a bee in her bonnet that I'm a right handsome feller. He's afraid he'll have me for a son-in-law before she can find out what an uncouth rascal I really am."

Jan's eyes snapped. "Did he say that?"

"No. But he sure meant it. Anyway, he's got it all figured out that the Brack holdings are now subject to several kinds of legal attachments. I can sue to recover my property, along with respectable damages to come out of Brack's loot. By the same token you can get the value of everything that has come out of the Three Toes mine. Half was yours by rights, and Brack's crooked bookkeeping will permit you to claim half of everything he salted into the deal. With damages added you'll get quite a tidy sum."

"But where does Mr. Moss come into this? And what does it have to do with your fatal charm for Vicky?"

He grinned amiably at her ironic tone.

"The general idea is that it will take a good lawyer or two to take care of our claims. Moss offers to push the whole deal for us if I'll pass up my golden opportunity to take advantage of his daughter's foolish infatuation. I quote his words, by the way."

She studied him a little disgustedly. "Would I sound catty if I advised you to take him up on it?"

"You would. But listen to the rest of the proposition. He figures I'll be a little better able to survive the loss of Vicky if I had another gal to take her place in my fickle affections. Which brings you into the deal again. For one thing, he points out, you're a good catch, being downright rich, and for another thing he thinks it would kill off some scandal. We did spend quite some time together in the hills, you know."

She advanced toward him threateningly, a hairbrush beating time to her angry words. "You get out of here! Of all the insulting things I've ever listened to that's the worst. Get out, I say!"

He chuckled mildly as she halted squarely in front of him. "I felt kinda the same way about it," he commented. "But I didn't let myself get sore at him for talking that way. He can't help it because he thinks like that — and he did do us a right good turn."

324

She seemed to be trying hard to see through his careful pose of solemnity. "Then you don't — ?"

"Sure I do." The owlish expression was still on his grimy countenance. "I was in favor of it even before you washed your face. I'm still in favor of it even with that hairbrush hanging over my head."

She took another step toward him as his grin broke through, but she dropped the hairbrush behind her.

We hope you have enjoyed this Large Print book. Other Thorndike, Wheeler, and Chivers Press Large Print books are available at your library or directly from the publishers.

For information about current and upcoming titles, please call or write, without obligation, to:

Publisher
Thorndike Press
295 Kennedy Memorial Drive
Waterville, ME 04901
Tel. (800) 223-1244

or visit our Web site at:

http://gale.cengage.com/thorndike

OR

Chivers Large Print
published by BBC Audiobooks Ltd
St James House, The Square
Lower Bristol Road
Bath BA2 3SB
England
Tel. +44(0) 800 136919
email: bbcaudiobooks@bbc.co.uk
www.bbcaudiobooks.co.uk

All our Large Print titles are designed for easy reading, and all our books are made to last.